BEFORE TIME
Ky-e-leron

I0552621

Dorothy Davies

BEFORE TIME
Ky-e-leron

ZADKIEL PUBLISHING

Zadkiel Publishing
An Imprint of Fiction4All
www.fiction4all.com

This Edition
Published 2018

Dedication

This book is dedicated with thanks to Ky-e-leron, the narrator for the cave dwelling Clan she eventually came to lead:

And Terry Wakelin, the rock and anchor in my life even from the other side of the divide. Never forgotten, beloved man, never forgotten.

I also want to mention Ken L Jones in Yucaipa, California, a long time friend; someone who has had tremendous input during the channelling of this book and Stuart Holland, publisher, friend and spiritual confidant here in the UK. Between the three of us we have relived much of this book, recalling our joint past lives at this time – a period of history which is before time.

Introduction to Before Time

I am Ky-e-leron. It means: I am Ky, daughter of Leron, shaman and leader of our group. We were many and shared the place wherein we dwelt. Many places and many demands did we make of the place wherein we lived, whilst being careful to give back our thanks and our gratitude with sacrifice, praise and words. Therein we created our living and therein we grew to know the truth of the wild world outside the cave dwellings, where the monsters lived and where we would one day die if we did not pay heed to them, every one of them.

Here now will I speak of those times, those days, those lives and those monsters. You need to know for your society now has no comprehension of our living and our lives, no comprehension of our struggles and our ability to overcome. You write of us in ways which make us look foolish, like cavemen with no thought. We were cavemen but oh, we thought.

The history of Man is ageless and endless. We called this book Before Time, 'we' being myself and the person writing it, for when we lived there was no such concept as seconds, minutes, hours, days, weeks, months or years as you live with now. We lived by the rising and setting of the sun and the span of the light during which we could work, hunt, build and gather.   We had but two 'seasons', Wake and Sleep. Sleep was the time when we sheltered and prepared for Wake; Wake was the time when we worked to be ready for Sleep. Compared with your time, life was simple then.

Read this if you really want to know of Cro-Magnon life and society. We were not the way you perceive us, we were not naked, hairy and ever carrying clubs.

We were not ignorant of speech, of morals, of society.

We were everything you are but with more, much more, for you would not survive the life we lived. If your world collapsed, if your wonderful technology failed, could you carry on?

My channel and I have discussed our lifestyle at great length, my story is told; her story is told.

Read on!

BEFORE TIME

Chapter 1 - Cro-Magnon Life

My channel asks: Tell me of your life.

Ky replies:

All life was for one thing: survival. We were there, we were people and we wanted to endure. We wanted to expand, go to newer lands; become one with that world outside. But the world outside was full of dangers, seen and unseen. We had to learn to fight, defend; go against that which we thought right if it was for the good of all rather than the good of one. We made ourselves one, one people through dance and song, combined work and sacrifice, breeding and dying and respecting all of it as part of the life we lived.

It was a life lived with spirits – of the caves where we lived, the earth which supplied all that we needed, the animals on which we depended, the afterlife, for we knew it existed, the great stars that we saw from our home on the dark nights when the moon hid herself from our view and left the glory of the glittering skies for us to gaze on and wonder at. Then the Shaman would visit those far distant places and bring back wisdom and advice to help us to live, knowledge of herbs and bark and grasses to heal our sick, taught us rituals and dances and chants to make us one people.

Ask of my life, dear one; I will tell what I can. You cannot know it all for you would not understand it all but we will see how far we can go.

My channel asks; what did you look like, what did you wear?

Ky replies:

Let me say first we were not the hairy, naked, grunting club-carrying caricatures I see in your books! In fact, this is an insult to our Clan and all other 'early' people, for we all had our own structured societies, ways of living and abilities.

So let me say first we were of medium height, we stood straight; we had very good eyesight and hearing which enabled us to hunt successfully. We had long hair, mostly dark, which some tied back with thongs made from sinews or strips cut from hides. Sometimes that went round their heads, sometimes it went round the hair itself. The men, when they matured, were somewhat hairy of body but that was concealed most of the time, concealed under the clothes we made. They grew beards and hair on their upper lip because to cut or shave it would mean spending time away from our many essential chores. There were other more important things to do than indulge in vanity. The men were mostly handsome, in my eyes anyway, having strong cheekbones and firm noses.

The women developed earlier than you do now, growing breasts and having wide hip structures from quite an early age. They let their hair grow and learned how to twist it up on their heads with wooden skewers when they were cooking, washing or tending the sick and wounded, so they did not annoy the patient. We women were, on the whole, dark eyed, soft of skin and seemed to be appealing to the men, judging by the amount of bonding which went on in our Clan, bonding that lasted for the lifetime of both persons. It was rare for a bonding to break, once made.

Women, from an early age, were taught the skills of cooking, sewing, tending the sick, the newborns, the animals and the young ones. They were taught the skills of what we must call love to be polite to your readers, dear channel; these were taught without embarrassment. They were a part of life, as much as the cooking and sewing and tending the sick were a part of life. We knew no other way.

All men, from an early age, were schooled in the art of weapons. They used throwing sticks, clubs were used only to finish off a kill; they had spears with which they practiced endlessly to ensure a clean kill if possible. They were all adept at using flint and stone to carve and cut, they trimmed bone to make combs and implements we could use in day to day living in our cave environment. They were very precise with their work, they made needles for us to sew with; it took great skill to make the hole for us to thread the sinews through. By 'us' I mean the women, for the men had other work, including their practice with spears and throwing sticks and teaching the younger ones the art of using these implements.

They were also good at stone throwing, something else they practiced all the time when they could leave the cave.

We wore tunics without sleeves in Wake, when the weather was warm, and tunics with sleeves and hoods when Sleep came, bringing its coldness with it. We wore long trousers and boots, mittens and long capes when the weather was very cold. All this we made, labouring over the sewing by the light of torches during the long dark hours of Sleep.

We will talk more about this later.

Does this paint a different picture to the ones you see in your books?

My channel asks; how did you speak to one another, what language did you use? Is it one we would recognise today?

Ky replies:

Your clever people insist that we had no language; that we grunted at one another. We know this, we see your books; we see your programmes. It is from these we – those of us who have chosen to communicate with you in your time – learned your language. We also use telepathy, so we are able to lift from you that which we need to communicate.

And there is your answer. We used what you call telepathy for the most part. We had language, not one you would understand but we had words for everything we used and ate and possessed and were. We had words for all emotions. We had words for every spirit we revered and worshipped. What we could not convey by words, we used our hands. Not sign language, but you can be expressive with your hands when added to words, you agree? And we conveyed much by thought.

So we did not grunt, we spoke. We did not use sign language but used our hands to add to the words we possessed. We had names and we used them. We had minds and we used them well.

We had our hierarchy, our society, which was rigid and held us together as a Clan. We were not the loosely associated group of hunter-gatherers, as you call us, roaming around naked, carrying clubs, hitting people over the head, dragging women around by their hair, grunting as we tore at lumps of meat over a fire. If I am truthful, and this book is designed to be just that, I have to say to you that we are all offended by this stereotyping of a complete race of people. The comment made to my channel, that ''they had nothing to do all day' shows the complete lack of understanding of 'prehistoric' life. We worked harder than you have ever done and still found time to worship the spirits, which is more than you do.

My channel asks: How did you divide your lives? We are used to days and weeks and seasons.

Ky replies:

We had two times. We had Wake and Sleep. Wake was warm with gentle rains and winds that did not destroy. Sleep was cold with violent storms and winds that tore everything apart. We devoted the whole of Wake to preparing for Sleep and devoted the whole of Sleep preparing for Wake. There was nothing else in our lives. Everything was done in those times and because of those times.

We were led by the Shaman, named Leron. He was my father. My mother I did not know: my life, her death. I was the first and only child of the Shaman, he took no other to wife; such was his love for my mother. He talked to me of her but what he said was for my ears and heart and none other. I will say only I look like her.

Leron would go into trance often; I will speak of this later. It is hard to know how to arrange the information so that you can absorb it and understand it. Suffice it to say for now he went into trance and in trance he was shown many things, many places, not all of this world. It was always in one such trance at the end of Sleep that he would be given the time when Wake began.

We must, of necessity, start somewhere so let us begin with

Chapter 2 - Wake

When the Shaman declared Wake had come, we took down the barrier at the cave entrance and burned it on the fire. We danced the freedom dance, freedom from darkness and cold, freedom from winds that blew too hard, freedom from snow that kept us locked inside. We all danced, every one of us, those who could just walk for they were newborn, those who could just walk for they were sick or wounded; those who could just walk for they were many Sleeps on this earth. We danced in rhythm round the fire which burned the old barrier and ended Sleep. We danced to the sound of the drum and the beating of hardened wood against the floor, a pounding rhythm that made blood grow warm and breath come fast and faces open in smiles that said we were newborn into Wake.

Then we dropped down where we were and mourned those who were not newborn into Wake, those whose journey had ended in Sleep, those who rested their bones in the sacred cave where they waited for us to join them. Those who we venerated for all they had done for us and for their protection during Sleep. For this was a dangerous time when the dark came early and stayed late, when the sounds from beyond the barrier were more than just hungry animals and rushing winds. The sounds were the hungry cries of restless spirits who sought the souls of man and woman to satisfy their craving to become human once again. We fought them with ritual and paint; we fought them with sigils, with chants, with herbs and with fire. And we fought them with the knowledge we gained through the Shaman's trance communications. We would sit in silence, no drums, no chants, waiting for the shaman to fly to other worlds, other times, other places and bring back the knowledge we needed to keep us safe. He never failed us. At times like that he was not my father, though we shared a part of the cave shelter and day to day living.

The sunrise after the great burning we all went out of the caves. Some went to cut fresh branches, new-grown and soft, and wove a new barrier which was left to dry and become hard. This we would put in the entrance through Sleep to keep out the wind, rain and snow. It had a small gap in one corner for bats to come and go. We shared our home with bats; they were our messengers, carrying our wishes and thoughts to the spirits of the trees and plants, of water and of earth.

Some began to search for new wood for the fire for it would be mostly gone. Sleep was always cold and hard and we needed much heat. New wood was needed to dry and be ready for the next Sleep as well as for cooking throughout Wake. The search for wood went on all through Wake. Whoever was out gathering, hunting, clearing, tending, looked for wood, bringing back small and large pieces which were stored and left to dry. We needed fuel all the time, to cook food, to provide firelight, to get ready for Sleep. Every person in the Clan worked to keep wood stocked up and we were never without.

Much food had to be found, food for all, rich food for those who were breeding, good food for those who danced the spirit dance and spoke with the spirits around us and guided us on our way, food for those who hunted, food for those who stayed and worked, for the caves had to be cleaned and purified, had to be cleansed and sanctified and our little ones, our new ones, kept safe from predators for they were our future.

Those who spoke with spirit were few, they were usually the very old, in our terms anyway, not yours. Those who had survived more Wakes and Sleeps than the rest of us had gained in wisdom and ability and could hear and speak to the spirits of the caves, of the trees, of the plants and all the other spirits we worshipped and worked for. We tried always to give these treasured people the finest cuts of the meats, the warmest hides, the first water drawn from the spring each time we went there. I had never given this a thought until now for it was so much a part of life it was never questioned.

The breeding and birthing animals were taken out to pastures of fresh new growth which helped them grow strong for the coming Sleep. The animals would almost run from the cave, such was their need to feel the sunshine and drink fresh water from the river, to graze the newborn grass and nibble at newborn leaves on bushes and trees. The young were carried out and placed with their group, the better to bond them for the long Sleep ahead. When the days became sharp and chill at the end of Wake, the animals would turn their heads to the cave entrance as if to ask if it were time to go back inside, even though once inside they were ill-natured and we had to take turns in guarding them against fighting and hurting one another. No matter that one of us would be hurt in the fight, horns can do damage, our stock was precious. Without them to provide milk and fresh meat during Sleep, we would be in difficulties. Some of us had the gift of talking to the animals and calming them when they wanted to fight. Once breeding started, much of their animosity calmed, it was the young ones who wanted to breed but who weren't ready which gave the most difficulty to us. It was then I would go and whisper to them, along with two young men who could talk them into quietness.

We will talk more of the animals later, when you ask other questions, as I know you will.

We spent the time of Wake outside as much as we could, hunting, fishing in the river, finding grasses and plants for us to use. The stronger men would gather honey and honeycombs from wild bees. I say stronger for it took courage, even with a thick hide covering on, to approach the nest and take the honey from the angry bees. We knew not who might die from a sting until it happened. The honey and the comb was stored and used in many different ways, to cook, to soothe and be part of salves and potions or just as a treat sometimes. It was much needed and the men knew this, so they got it for the rest of us.

Wake was a time of rains, of sunshine, of births of animals and our own newborns, of fun and laughter in the work we had to do, for there was always time for tricks and things to make us laugh. The old ones benefited from the sunshine, from the warmth and would spend time in the entrance to the caves, busy weaving baskets and sewing clothes and watching over the little ones who ran hither and thither, enjoying the freedom that they could not have in the time of Sleep.

The men worked at their skills with throwing sticks and spears and the throwing of stones.

The women also wove baskets and sewed to help them out during Sleep, when there often seemed more to do than Wake, if that be possible. Yes it is. I just realised – we tended to take so much for granted. During Wake the animals were free to wander and feed, during Sleep we had to tend to them and were endlessly carrying water for their needs or to clean the caves where they lived, to keep them supplied with torches so they could see. Yes, there was more work during Sleep. In Wake we could sit outside and sew as well, no need for torches.

Wake was freedom.

Chapter 3 - Sleep

As with Wake, the Shaman would tell us when Sleep was to begin. As it was, we prepared for Sleep all through Wake. We stacked animal fodder and food in the caves; we collected a plentiful supply of honey, fruits, berries, nuts and as much firewood as we could carry and store, we cleaned the caves, especially where we stored food and the dead, we made arrangements for the animals, making pens to keep them safe from one another. During Wake we scraped and cleansed hides for our use so that during Sleep we could turn them into whatever was needed, everything from shrouds to foot coverings. We made endless torches, too. Every family group burned several of these every day so there was a never-ending need for them, for we had to have light. We had to have torches for the animals too, so they did not go blind in the darkness of the caves. So many things to think of; so many things to do. A hunt during Wake could take some days, bringing back fallen trees could take many days but was worth it for we needed the wood for many different things, building and burning.

The Shaman would say, "Sleep comes soon," and the work would multiply, our last chance to be in the cool sunshine, the cool winds, the freshness of the outside world where the leaves were busy changing to browns and golds, where the sky looked polished, just as we polished the glittery shiny stones we sometimes found in the river and brought in to make into something pretty to wear. We would see the birds frantically finding the last food for themselves; wild life eating all they could and we would know the Shaman was right, Sleep was upon us.

And then the morning would come when he would say 'it is done'. We would bring the animals into the caves, make sure we had all the chickens safely inside, that there was nothing outside the cave that should be inside and then we would go out for what felt like the last time and then pull the big barrier across the entrance and be grateful for it, for the heat would start to build and we would realise how cold we had become in the short time before Sleep came.

It was almost a relief to sit by the fire for a few moments and gaze at one another and think: it was a good Wake, we did so much. We could, at that point, overlook the small fact that within a short time we would detest the sight of the barrier and sometimes each other, as we were in such close confines. But this was surface, below that we were one and we knew it. We were the Clan.

Young ones who had already lived through one Sleep were looking around, perhaps wondering what they would do with themselves until Wake came. Younger ones who had only lived through Wake were wide-eyed with astonishment at the closing in, the huge barrier and the need for torches all the time.

I have not mentioned the other animals before now, so let me say we had our dogs, large hairy animals that helped in the hunts that went on and who protected us from ravaging wild animals.

We had cats that lived with us in the caves. They were larger than the animals you have now as pets. Their work was to keep the rats and other scavenging animals from taking our food and destroying our hides. We could not have managed without these creatures with us.

The dogs would be by the fire, lying down with a sigh of contentment. Their working days were through for a while, no hunting, no rushing here and there, just time to rest and be and let us groom them and take their fur for ourselves. The cats would be by the fire but watching and soon enough they would be prowling the caves, looking for vermin to entrap and keep us and our precious supplies safe. We suffered very little damage and loss thanks to these remarkable animals.

There would be some sunny days still and we would ease the barrier aside and slide out, getting yet more firewood for there was never enough, more grass and more plants and nuts and fruits from the trees and bushes nearby, not going very far for fear of sudden rainstorms that could chill someone through and give them illnesses by their very coldness. Sometimes this fine weather would go on and we would think the Shaman had it wrong, but we would say nothing, just made the most of the fine days.

And then the weather would change. At first it would be just cold winds, then the whitening of the ground and cold, cold nights and then the rain and the snows would come.

The rain would often flood the valley below us; then we did not go out for fear of losing our footing in the mud. The rain brought a cold we did not have with the snow, a cold that caused the old to mumble with the pain in their joints and we would need healing herbs and salves to ease them. These were made by those with knowledge of such things. I made many a salve and many a potion during the long days of Sleep.

The snow, when it came, would oft times stack itself up against the barrier and we would be constantly climbing up to create a narrow flight path for the bats with whom we shared the caves, not that they used it all the time but we could not entrap them with us. That would have been unfair. We tolerated the small amount of bitter coldness of the outside coming in to allow them their way out to the world in which we could not walk at times, not without risking our very lives. We could feed ourselves, they could not.

The snow had a benefit, it made the caves warmer; the heat stayed inside as the snow froze against the barrier and made it impregnable, apart from the small place for the bats. I loved those fleeting mysterious creatures that roosted in the high parts of the caves and did not bother us, they had learned to swoop above us and go out when they needed. Their droppings were carefully scraped up and used as fuel, along with the droppings of the animals. We wasted nothing. It added to the firewood and that was good.

You are going to ask, so I will say, yes – sometimes the young would decide to go out in the snow to search for fresh food, to release their energies and yes, sometimes the young would not return. The sadness was that it was usually the young males who went and we needed young males for bonding, for parenting, for work. But who can control the energies of the young when their hearts are full of bravery and their minds full of the thrill of challenging the weather during Sleep? The Shaman would forbid them to go but so many times they would ignore his dictat and go anyway.

Their names were eternally engraved in our hearts.

My channel asks: When there were bright sunny days during Sleep, when the snow did not stack itself so high against the barrier, did you go outside as a group?

Ky replies:

You are right, we did that. We looked for those days to release our boredom from being inside. Had there been more days like that, maybe the young males would not have found the need to go when it was dangerous to go. We would ease the barrier to one side and slide through, carefully. We ran, we hunted, for the dogs loved to romp through snow and see what they could find for us. We gathered wood and plant life to add to all that already stored within the caves. There could never be enough for we never knew when Sleep would end. We knew it would, it always ended but we never knew when. So we gathered what we could when the chance was given. The bitter winds would bring down branches, even a tree or two, which could be taken back to the caves and added to the store, the ever needed store. Without light, without heat we would not have survived more than a day. I cannot say how important this was to us without sounding as if I am constantly repeating myself.

On those bright days we walked out of the caves and into the bitter sunshine, feeling the coldness bite the skin and knew it to be good, cleansing; needful. We could not always wash and sometimes...

I would not have you think we were unclean because of lack of consideration for others. It was the endless work. Water had to be carried from its underground pathway. We carried water endlessly for the animals, for the young, for the old, for cooking, for cleansing the caves – we had to ensure our wastes were washed away when we could not go outside – you can see it was a big task for us, as big as the need to store wood and other fuel for the fires. To go outside and be refreshed by soft rains – some days brought soft rains – was good. We could clean ourselves and our clothes.

When we were cold, cold to our very insides, we would go back in and those who were tending the great fire would welcome us, for it would be their turn to go out into the sunshine and be cleansed. And although we were ready to be warm again, we would be a little sorrowful that we were not out there, breathing clean air and smelling clean smells, not smoke, old food and people.

You are perceptive, my channel, to think of this.

Chapter 4 – Daily Living

My channel asks: tell me about your living arrangements.

Ky replies:

We were cave dwellers. Here I want to take a moment to tell you of the cave as seen from the outside. The entrance was not wide, as most people seem to think, a great curve, but very tall and narrow. This had many purposes. First, the stone of the mountain itself made a strong barrier against the weather which battered it. Second, a narrow entrance was easier to barricade. We made a rigid barrier, as I said, from green branches which then dried. This was put into the space, the entrance, for Sleep, leaving a small gap at the very top. This enabled the bats to come and go as they wished and the smoke to leave the cave, if the wind was not blowing directly at us. Smoke rises, so it drifted out of the top of this tall narrow barrier. It also gave us a lot of wall space to use, for there were many of us. I hope this is clear, it goes against your usual image but it makes better sense, I do believe.

We all had our separate living areas and sometimes our own cave. The caves themselves divided the Clan into its areas; there were formations which naturally created a wall or barrier between each group. The largest cave always went to the Shaman and his family, after that it was by seniority, the Elders first. Some had their own cave;

others had an area which was theirs by the way it was formed.

It would be surprising to modern people how a small outcrop of rock could make the difference, make a barrier respected by all. We lived in a relatively open way, but we respected others and their need for family privacy and so we saw these small outcroppings as larger than they were. No one entered another family's area without standing at the 'entrance' and knocking, either by stamping a foot or banging with a stave on the floor. Then they would be bidden to enter. No matter what the family were doing, they would permit others to enter and take part in their meal, their prayers; their story time. It would be a while that the person would stay and then they would go, to allow the family to go to their beds.

Now let me tell you of our arrangements. We had stools which we made from hides and wood that was straight and strong. We had our containers to fetch water, food, to store herbs and berries, things like that. We had few clothes so there was no need to hang anything anywhere.

Our sleeping platforms were built of branches and straw and dried grasses and covered in thick hides and kept off the floor, even though the floor was covered in hides, the better to protect our feet from the cold, cold stone. We had a pillow of dried grass, stuffed into a small portion of hide and we had hides to cover us, the fur turned inward for warmth. We had hoods for our heads and almost all of our faces, for even with such coverings our faces and heads grew cold. We had coverings for our hands and feet, too. We slept warm like that if the cold was not too intense. If it was, we were very cold for the hides stopped the heat of the fire reaching us.

We all shared the fire in the middle of the great central cave. It sent heat out for all of us, warmed the air we breathed, dried our clothes; cooked our food. Each family had a flat stone in the ring around the fire where they cooked meat and breads. No one touched another's stone or another's food.

The walls were wet through the breath of so many people. I cannot tell you how many, we had no counting method, but there were a lot. We put nothing against the walls.

We had torches for light. We made these by stuffing grasses and moss into horns and lighting them from the fire. They were put into holes in the walls of the cave, not holes we had made, that was forbidden, as I will tell you later. These were holes that were there naturally. We utilised all that we could without damaging the shelter which surrounded us.

We were roused by the Shaman's call each day to help rebuild the fire, feed the animals, feed the people, fetch fresh water to drink, wash away the wastes which had collected in one corner in rough baskets or allowed to flow under the barrier and out. We sent water down the rock to wash it away.

We tended the sick and elderly who could not leave their beds. They needed help to dispose of their wastes, to intake food and water where they could still do such a thing, to cleanse them if we could. It was then we would find the ones who did not make it to morning, the ones who would not see another day.

When someone did not wake in the morning, the Elder Women would assemble around the sleeping place of that person and there they would begin a low, almost chilling chant. It was almost under the breath at first, hard to hear and yet – and yet every one of us knew the chant, knew it as well as we knew our names. We would join in and call for the spirit of the dead to be at peace and to wait for the great Wake when we would all be one again together. We sang that we would not forget their name or their life.

It slowly and steadily got louder and louder. At some point which none could pinpoint but was always the same, the Elder Men would step forward and lift the hide on which the person lay. With great dignity they would carry this, slowly and carefully, to the cave of the dead, one that was safe and secure at the very end of our complex of caves, where no animals went and no predator could enter. There they were laid on the cold floor for then it no longer mattered. We would cross their hands at their stomachs and close their eyes if they were open. Everyone associated with that person would follow; the rest of the Clan would walk after them. The chant would be louder and if this is possible, sadder than it was before. There would be tears. There would be beating of the body with fists to try and ease the hurt. There would be sympathy in the eyes but not the arms of the others; it was for each of us to stand alone in our grief. It was our way.

There was not room for the whole Clan to gather in the cave but they would be outside, still hearing the repeated chant. We knew it well. We had heard it many a time and more. The chant was as much a mourning for our loss as a call to the person to rejoin us as a spirit. One of the women would call out, a sound like,

Yaaaraaahhhh!

We would then begin stamping hard on the cave floor, accompanying the chant. This intense call or cry for our loss would go on for a very short time and then we would stop. All of us together. I never did know how or why we did it so perfectly but we did. The silence was as intense as the chant and the stamping. Then we would turn as one and go back to our home and carry on our lives as always; knowing the spirit would return when they were ready.

The family of the dead one would gather their most precious possessions, beads they wore, a knife they used, their flint, whatever was precious and take them back to the dead and put it in their hands so they did not feel bereft without it.

Later, the body would be stitched into a shroud of hide but not before we gave their spirit time to leave the body and become used to its new existence. I must also say here that should we need to open the shroud, we would know which person was treasured in that way by the item they had in their hands. The item was doubly important for those reasons.

When Wake came, one of our first tasks was to bury our dead in the earth that birthed us, to return them to their natural home. Until then, they were safe in their own cave in our lives. We waited for them and they never failed us. They always came back.

My mother was buried with her favourite possessions, a necklace of stones found in the rocks, stones which sparkled, a bowl carved for her from bone and other items which were precious to her. She was not in the ground; she was in a far distant cave where those of stature are laid, shamans and shamans' partners and siblings. I should be there too but I was not to die in the conventional way and I was never recovered.

She came back often, but to my father, not to me. It was as if we had not bonded before she passed, maybe she never saw me, I will never know because it is not something you can ask a spirit, it would be unfair. 'Why did you not come to me?' sounds like an accusation and I would not do that to the person who gave me life.

I would ask that you forgive the longer answer than perhaps you sought, my channel, but I needed first to explain the areas of the caves which were given over to the individual families. I trust you have followed the way we thought, the way we were with one another. Respect was everything. If a dispute arose, the Shaman tried to settle it. No one questioned his authority to do so. Disputes were few; we had to learn to tolerate one another, especially during Sleep.

The barrier was necessary for our warmth and protection but was also symbolic; it also kept out the spirits we did not want attacking us during the time when we were so close together. It was easy for problems to arise, for tempers to ferment and then explode.

We have much to discuss, I know at this moment your mind is bursting with questions, but we must work our way through our complex lives. You would have the same problem were you to try and describe your lives to visitors from other worlds who would not understand.

My channel asks: you talk of certain special people having their role to play in these ceremonies; did that apply to all of life?

Ky replies:

Yes, it did. First I must tell you of our society, how it is structured. Below the Shaman, in importance, were the Elder Men of the Clan. They were not there by age: they were there by wisdom, by work, by understanding of the natural world in which we lived. There were a group of them. When one passed on, another naturally came from the Clan to take the place. It was not a 'choice', it was a happening. Is this possible to be understood? A group of people. One morning one of them does not wake. The others take him to the dead cave. There is now a gap in the group. During the day someone will walk in and join the group. No words will be spoken; nothing will be given or received. It just happens, as if they are called. It has never failed to be right. There was never a disagreement of any kind among the Elder Men.

Below them, if we are thinking structure, are the Elder Women. They were the ones responsible for stitching the dead into their shrouds; it was from them the chosen ones come to create the robes for the Shaman. They helped at the time of childbirth, they helped with calming those who had a first bleed and were afraid of coupling. They helped with the birthing of animals if there were problems. They nursed the sick and the wounded. We, the younger ones, relied on the Elder Women for everything. I did, more than the others, as I had no mother to turn to.

You will want to know one more thing; I know that, so let me say it before you ask: when we women began our blood flow, we used the softest of mosses held in place with cords. I could draw them for you but I cannot describe them for you without going into such personal detail it would be embarrassing for us both. I am sure you can work it out.

There, now it is said and we can move on.

Below them were the Leaders. They were both men and women, we made little difference between them when it came to leading, only differentiating for times of childbirth and death, for it needed the sensitivity of a woman to do those things rather than the clumsiness of the men. I say this knowing well that they understood their role and stood back at such times. Leaders took us out of the caves during Sleep into the bigger world on those fine sunny days we spoke of. Leaders searched for the reckless young who broke out during snow and did not return. Leaders were everywhere and we needed them, too.

The rest of us fell into our roles as we were called: we had those who tended the animals with skill and knowledge acquired we knew not how, those who knew where to search for herbs, roots and nuts we knew not how, those who knew what to do when things happened. You know yourself how you turn to someone, just knowing they will have the answer.

My channel asks; what of the injured? You speak of the elderly and the sick. You do not speak of the injured.

Ky replies:

Again you are perceptive, my dear channel. The seriously injured, the badly wounded, did not survive. Those wounds would turn a terrible foreboding yellow and black, there would be a terrible smell too and we would know, as did that person, there was no hope for them. I confess to you now that sometimes we ended the life of that person to save the suffering as the poison got hold and sent them into tremors and convulsions. We could not allow our fellow man to suffer in that way. The Shaman would quietly end their lives and we would know, by the gratitude shown through the spirit, that it was what that person wanted but did not want to ask, for fear of our incurring the wrath of other spirits. We knew this would not happen but they were always in fear of this.

My channel asks, we have spoken now of illness and death, of wounds and of loss, can we now speak of the newborn? What happened with those who were not right, who were deformed, for example. Were there ceremonies for the new arrivals in the Clan? How were they named?

Ky replies:

This is a good subject on which to talk for a while. We as a Clan welcomed the newborn. When the mother announced she was to bring forth a newborn, she was taken into the heart of the Clan, she was given nourishing foods, kept warm, given 'newborn' gifts, the softest hides for the life to come, a cradle, pendants, bracelets; rattles for the child. These all came from the women of the Clan and, as many make this announcement during Sleep, we were kept busy with making the gifts for the newborn and the mothers. There was little time during Sleep to rest. There is always so much to do.

When the time approached, the mothers would go to the small cave away from the main areas, so that if they screamed and cried, it did not touch the hearts of the men and the younger ones who had yet to mature to that point. No one wished them to be scared of their future, no one wished the men to regret having created a newborn. The men found something to do to distract them from thinking of the woman giving birth and, as I said, there was always so much to do that was not difficult for them.

The Elder Women went with the mothers and some of us, I include myself here, began the task of carrying water and food to them so they did not have to leave the ones they were tending. Chants were said that the newborns would survive and the mothers would survive, too. Spirits were called upon to see the mothers through the ordeal of birth and we asked that both mother and newborn would survive. It can take a very long time to push the newborn out; it can be a quick thing. Some mothers left before we had a chance to bring the first lot of water to the cave, some left before the first food arrived, some were there for two or three visits with food and water and some never left.

One by one the living mothers left the cave, carrying their newborn. The look of joy they wore when this happened was enough to endear them to everyone, no matter their status in the Clan. The fathers, even as they worked, watched anxiously as each new mother arrived back in the main area to show their newborn to the rest of us. Then they were reunited with the fathers and went to their own area, there to tend and welcome and think of a name for their newborn.

The remaining fathers watched and waited whilst busying themselves with tasks, wondering when their newborn would arrive. As the daylight went to night and sometimes back to daylight and night again, so these fathers lost their look of excited expectancy and began to look apprehensive and then afeared.

Sometimes the woman left the cave without a newborn in her arms. She walked with her head down and her eyes all but closed, she walked with the care and grief weighing her down. Then we saw the father go to her and hold her and say next time it will be good. They would walk away and we, who were waiting with them, say nothing for there was nothing can be said to heal the hearts of those who lost their newborn.

When the Elder Women finally emerged, the fathers who were left knew that their wait was over, that their chosen one would not be returning to them. A newborn could survive the mother but it had to be given to another new mother to feed and care for. The look of devastation on the faces of the men who were left without their partner was sad beyond bearing. Every partnering was made with joy; every parting was greeted with the sadness and the searing grief of loss. If the loss was of the newborn as well, the grief was a double blow to the waiting father. Some did not survive the loss; they went out into the world and did not return. Their names, as with those of their partners, are carved in our hearts.

You asked about the arrival of newborns with physical problems. Those we had to consider carefully. Was the problem so great the child could be of no use to the Clan in the future? Or was the problem one that could be overcome with help and some thought? These problems were brought to the Shaman for his decision on whether the deformed one would be allowed to live. It seems harsh but every member of the Clan knew that every mouth had to be taken into account and that person had to grow to become a useful member of the Clan.

You have not asked, dear channel, about those who were born with the blank face of those who had no true brain. There was no question with them; they were quietly disposed of, to use an expression that should not offend. Those with such difficulties had no place in the Clan for we could not allocate helpers to be with them at all times. Every pair of hands was needed for us to get through the Wakes and Sleeps ahead of us. We had to be cruel to ensure the survival of the others.

The time of Wake was a time of great happiness, for we were able to leave the caves and take on a new life. But it was also a time of great sadness for those who had not survived to see Wake again. Those who were old and tired, those who were sick, those who did not survive the birthing, all these we held in our hearts. Some Wakes began with being busy with many burials. No. I am wrong. All Wakes began with being busy with many burials. So many did not survive Sleep.

You asked about naming our newborns, dear channel. Names were important, they signified so much; who we were; who we belonged to, so none were mistaken.

Ky means spirit. The name was given for I was expected to take on the mantle of being the Shaman's assistant as I grew and learned and was able to be part of the sacred secret ceremonies.

Others chose the name for their child for what they wanted the child to be, leader, painter, hunter, carver and, for every one of them, their name was linked to the father, as mine was. A simple way of knowing who belonged to which father.

The names were chosen after the newborn had been in this world for a few daylight and darkness times, for nothing could be hurried. The wrong name could lead the newborn into a life that was not right for them.

The names were chosen after the parents spoke with the Shaman about the direction for their child. They gave their thoughts, he gave his knowledge from the spirit world and then the name was given. The child was carried to the great fire and the name announced to all so it could be engraved on the hearts of everyone. How proud we all were then, how proud that the Clan had another living member to take part in our future. There were many such wonderful namings; it helped us cope with the grief of the ones who were lost.

We were a close and caring community. I know in your world you use these words as if they are of nothing. For us they meant everything. If we said to someone 'I care for you' they meant in every way. Care of them when sick, when well, in good and bad Wakes and Sleeps, when food was short or water hard to get, no matter what, the words were meant and the meaning of the words was kept.

My channel asks; how were the children reared? How were they carried, what toys did they have; what education did they have?

Ky replies:

Our newborns were held close in special slings round the mother's neck. Sometimes, if the mother had a bad birth experience and was weak, the father would carry the newborn for a time. Either way the bond was made, the newborn treasured and cared for, carried inside hides lined with fur and wool. As with the women who experienced blood loss regularly, the newborns were given soft mosses to catch their water and their wastes. They wore loose garments of the finest hides, so soft they could be wrapped up and held in one hand.

For toys they had carved animals, wood or bone, rattles cleverly carved so that the thing which rattled was made inside its cage rather than being put inside. They also had wooden bells, although I have to say sometimes the clanging of wooden bells could become a little too much…

Balls were made by binding mosses with sinews and letting them dry, then wrapping more moss and more sinews around them until a reasonable sized ball was made. These would last some time, a well made ball would last the whole of Wake, being kicked or thrown around outside. New ones would be made for the newborns, by then small children, to roll around the cave floor during Sleep.

The carved animals were works of art. We had many skilled carvers who made a whole range of animals for every child in the Clan. All this was done after the day's work was through, when the firewood had been stocked, the animals tended, the grasses and plants for food brought in, the kills from the hunt stored in the cave or set to cook for us to eat. There was always work: curing hides, making harnesses for animals who towed trees back to the caves, making cradles for newborns, making… the list could go on forever. What you take for granted, what you go to shops to buy, we had to make somehow with what we had available. And we did and we lived well.

You asked about education, dear channel. The children were taken on hunts from an early age; they were taught how to behave around the animals from the moment they could walk. They were told of the spirits we worship, of the need to respect the spirit of the caves, to respect one another and not cause problems. There were always minor disputes with the children until they learned possessions belong to one person, they were not there for another to take without permission, that jealousy has no place in a community and that everyone, every single person big and small, had their part to play in the survival of the Clan.

You thought, but did not ask, where did the moss come from? After all, we used a lot of it.

I told you earlier the walls were constantly wet with the bodies of so many people in one place. We had stones placed all around the walls. Moss grew on the stones. We carefully scraped off what we needed and let it grow back again. There was always moss to harvest.

My channel asks; what about the moss and other plants? Was the moss used to make potions and salves for those who were sick or wounded? My feeling is that it was.

Ky replies:

Yes, we grew moss for our potions and salves as well as for our bodily use. Moss is a determined thing, it grows in many places and clings with strength to stones and crevices; anywhere it can grow. We admired it for its strength and used it for its potency as well as its softness. We harvested other plants during Wake, some with special berries; some with special flowers. The Shaman told us which ones to collect and we brought them back in baskets, trying not to touch them very much so that we did not take the strength and vitality from the stems and leaves. The flowers were dried and crushed, the berries were stored and used as fresh as

41

we could get them. If they dried out, we crushed them and used the powder.

I say 'we'. I mean the Elder Women who were entrusted with the making of potions and salves, which were crushed and powdered plants mixed with honey from wild bees. Such a mixture can be put on a wound or a rash or a sore of some kind and it would bond with the body and start the healing. Many a shallow wound recovered after being coated with honey and herbs.

We mixed herbs and honey with water heated by the fire for those who coughed too much and damaged their chests by doing this. The mixture would ease the cough and help them sleep, part of the recovery. We had a cave put aside for the storing of plants, berries, honey, baskets full of fresh smelling and potent flowers and leaves – it was a pleasure to visit but we visited it as little as possible. A double thick curtain of hides shielded it from day to day passing by; sealing in as much as possible all that was right and good so that when the Elder Women entered to make their potions, it was as good as it could be.

With their skills, some wounded people survived, but I have to say that it was those who had chest wounds, or stomach, or genitals or back, these were the ones who did not survive. A spear thrust to the leg – yes, it happened once by accident – was enough to cause a wound so deep no amount of honey and herbs could stop it turning that terrible colour and giving off that terrible smell. But lesser wounds, those we got from day to day collisions with the animals, with trees, with the fire if we were not careful, from falls on sharp rocks, these could be cured most of the time.

Those who grew hot and we could not cool them for some time, they did not always survive. But we did what we could with what we had and the many who recovered showed that we could heal.

My channel asks: for those who are left without a partner after the birthing, for those who are left alone when someone passes on from wounds or illness, how do they find another partner?

Ky replies:

In a group like the Clan, there are always single people who are happy to start a new bonding. Those we lose in childbirth, in hunting accidents, in illness and other happenings, are never forgotten but the survival of the Clan is everything and those who are left start to look around for a partner straight away. It is for the benefit of all that a new bonding is made as soon as possible. It will not be the same for either of them, this we know and this we understand but we also know that time does heal all things and the two who come together make a new bonding that often lasts until again one or other of them is taken home to the spirit world. It was a constantly changing situation, for there were many things which took our people home. It was the only way we could survive and continue as a clan, as a people. It was understood by all and never caused any difficulties.

My channel asks: Can you tell me more about the way you carried water and other items? How did you make these carrying containers?

Ky replies:

We made our containers from wood and from hide. We wove baskets from reeds growing in the river but these were not strong enough for water, these we used for berries, herbs, nuts, seeds and small items like that. They were made by the women; the men were busy with carving. It was nothing to do with 'men do one task and women another'. We shared the work equally. We women wove baskets, sometimes with covers, sometimes not. The men carved wood into bowls and containers for things like honey. We used the liquids we found in trees to line the bowls and containers. When it dried it made a coating that stopped the water escaping through any cracks in the wood, or soaking into the wood. There were certain trees we used and others we did not. Clan lore said which were good for us and which were not good for us: we never questioned why this tree and not another, we just took what we needed and gave thanks to the spirit of earth and all that was in it for the gifts we had.

The reason the work divided that way is simple: the men had stronger hands to do the wood carving and the stone carving which I will tell you about soon. The women had faster lighter hands to do things like weaving and making torches, all the women could make torches quicker than any man. They used to have contests and the women always won. The men eventually gave up...

The work went on as endlessly as the making of torches, toys, clothes and other items for the Clan. Everyone made something all the time.

We had a way of making containers from the hides; we would cut a round piece from a hide and then make holes in the edge. Here we would thread sinews, fine sinews, and draw the whole thing up together, after it had been coated several times with the liquid from the trees. We could make small ones like this or large ones. We all had a lot of them and used them to carry water, milk and honey when the brave ones got the honey for us from the angry bees. We would hang these from points of rock in the caves until we needed them.

We had stone containers for the animals' drinking water, they needed much more than we did. The Elder men would choose large pieces of stone from the river, ones which already had a hollow in it made by the ever running, ever talking water and they would work at this with obsidian and flint and other stones, chipping away endlessly until a deep hole was made in the stone. Then they would carry this into the caves where the animals stayed all Sleep and set it in place. Our job was to make sure it was always clean, that there was no green growing in it, which would hurt the animals. We needed a lot of these stones and the work was arduous and unrewarding; it took so long to make each one. The good thing about it was, once a stone had been cut out in this way, it would last forever, unlike the wooden and hide ones which needed renewing all the time. So in some ways it could be seen as rewarding. The men would take turns at working on it as it was too much for one and of course every man had other duties to carry out all the time. But we managed. Somehow.

Our days were not endless but at times they felt as if they were.

My channel asks, what about your clothes? How were they made and what did you wear?

Ky replies:

We were experts at making clothes. We knew about needles and could stitch hides together to make warm clothing and other items to help us through Sleep. We would take scraped hides and make of them trousers, tunics, capes, footwear, hats and mittens. When the hides were new, they were stiff but with wear they became soft. We made pillows and bedding for ourselves and for those who were not capable of making their own. I see from your books you people think we went around wearing no clothes, that we were very hairy people, that we could endure cold without covering. This is absolute nonsense. No one could survive the time of Sleep with their bodies uncovered, for the snow would lie deep for many, many days and the bitter cold would have killed all of us if we were not covered up. Yes, we had the fire but you cannot stay by a fire all the time. You had to go to other caves: you had to tend to the sick, the newborn, the injured, the dying. You had to collect water and bring food to the animals and take away the dung the animals produced. There was much work to do all the time, as I have said before. Life was not easy for us. If we were unclothed our lives would have been impossible. It is hard to believe that sensible people could imagine we went without clothing but then, I see the many silly errors they make when they talk of what you call prehistoric people. I have to say they know nothing.

I do know they have little to work with but oh, why do they assume so much? We were not one step up from animals, we were human beings, living, working, struggling to survive without all that you have in your modern world in the way of comforts and aids to living. What we needed we had to make. What we could not make we went without.

Nothing was wasted. Nothing. When an animal was killed, we used every part of it. The meat was for food, the hide was for covering, the sinews were for sewing, fishing, tying things together or securing them against the spirit of the wind. We used them when constructing the barrier for the cave entrance to keep the wood together. We used them to bind the bones or horns together which formed the torches we used to light our caves. The bones were used in many ways, to make torches, as I said; to form into weapons to fight the foes – for we had enemies, even as you do. They were also good for sacrificing the animals we needed to eat. The bones could be carved and often were to make decorative items for the Shaman or the ladies to please them when they brought forth the newborns. I cannot think of anyone in the Clan who could not carve wood or bone and make something wonderful for someone to keep. Sadly, bone and wood have not survived the years until discovery of our homes. Natural things do not. Stone does but not many were skilled in stone carving as we had inadequate tools for such work. A few knew how to use one stone to sculpt another but really, just a few where everyone else could carve the softer things.

We appreciated beauty. We would gaze in awe at a sunset, at a star-thrown sky, at a full heavy moon hanging low, the colours of a sunrise, the glory of flowers and herbs, new-grown trees and early Wake grasses, the colour of water as it ran down its chosen course to what we were told was the sea. We would admire the robes created for the Shaman with their intricate traceries and decorations. We would admire the beautiful women who walked among us whilst knowing that those with the plainer faces were just as valuable to the Clan as the beautiful ones and, as the Shaman whispered to me one night, would decay just as fast when they were gone to the afterlife. Us women would sigh over the handsome men who walked among us, whilst knowing the fluids of those who were less favoured was just as valuable and these less favoured ones were more inclined to be loyal, trusting and caring of a woman. It was easy to be distracted by outward appearances, it was better to see what lies beyond the smile and decide whether the person would care for you throughout your life, see to your needs, give you children to perpetuate the race, be a living essential part of the Clan, be loving and trusting of his woman, ensure she was kept warm throughout Sleep and safe throughout Wake.

If I could explain: it was a general feeling amongst the Clan that Sleep was a time for keeping warm, for the caves were cold and the spirit of the wind seemed determined to find a way in and chill us with its iced fingers and Wake brought its own dangers, for the moment we went outside we would find snakes that bit, insects that stung and caused swellings and sometimes death, we would see accidents taking our loved ones from us, animals that would turn and cause injury from which our loved ones would not recover. Sometimes the golden rays of the sun would be so hot everything would be dry and would burn and we would be burnt along with it for our skin would turn red and come away in strips and we would be troubled by nights of not sleeping and not rebuilding our strength for the work to be done before Sleep. Wake was a time of danger. Sleep was a time of cold.

The good thing was, Sleep was a time of storytelling and the Shaman's trance visits to other places for then we had enough to satisfy our enquiring minds. Sleep was a time for love in all its forms, to create new life and strengthen the bonds between partners. Sleep was when the newborns were started and new bondings were beginning to show themselves. I will talk on this shortly.

Wake was a time of enjoyment, of brighter daytimes and warmer nights, of watching things grow, plants, bushes, trees, newborn animals, birds shedding shells, newborn people learning to be grown up but failing because they were so small and so delightful and such a pleasurable thing to watch. Everyone took responsibility for newborns; they were surrounded with love, protection, attention and yet more love, for they were our future. We never stopped being aware of that. Newborn parents could go about their lives knowing their offspring were in the best hands imaginable, the hands of the Clan.

The bonding of the young began in Sleep and was carried into Wake. The Shaman would be observing who was attracted to who and would have quiet words with the family of both to find out if they approved or not. If they did not approve, then the young would be advised to look elsewhere. It did not happen often, I have to say, mostly we found our true love our own way and those around us were content to let us go there. After that it was emphasised that if they bonded, it was for life and their happiness and their health and their future was in their hands, they had to take care of one another as well as being part of the Clan. Then everyone worked to find them their space. This was created by someone dying and going to the spirit world. Everything they left would be burned on the great fire as part of the cleansing of the space. It meant that the newly bonded couple could start afresh, not take on the memories of the person who had left us. This was an essential part of our teachings.

The man would build the new things they needed, sleeping platform and whatever else his new woman wanted. This is why it went into Wake, there was much to do and during Sleep it wasn't easy to get outside for the wood and the hides and the stuffing needed for everything. This was a good thing; it gave the young a chance to really get to know one another, working together in their space with whatever they could find or were given by the Clan from inside the caves. The bonding really started then and was consummated in Wake with a joyous ceremony which we all attended. There was chanting and dancing and much feasting and merry making. We showered them with leaves to give them fertility, with flowers to give them beauty and with pungent herbs to give them love.

Sometimes we had many bonding couples, sometimes we had few. It depended on whether Sleep had been hard and we had not all come through, or perhaps there were not enough young females who had experienced their first blood, or simply they were not ready for the commitment.

We liked it so much when there were many, for then the celebrations would go on for some days. We would have to work twice as hard to make up for the time spent celebrating but it was worth it, worth every part of the aching body and the weariness with which we faced the days afterwards. Celebrations were few and far between, we had to make the most of every joyful occasion to lift ourselves from the routines of the days, from the work of Wake taking us into Sleep and the work of Sleep taking us into Wake.

I know well you experience the same feelings, for your lives, despite not being divided as ours were, are driven by the same needs: food, shelter, clothing; warmth. Nothing changes.

My channel asks: what was it like living in the caves? Was it noisy; was it very smelly; were there problems?

Ky replies:

Unless you have lived in a cave it is hard to describe but I will try.

First, let me talk of the noise. It was incessant but you learned to live with it. The first noise was the fire endlessly talking to us as it consumed wood, scraps of hide left over from making clothes, animal droppings, anything that could burn was given and the fire consumed it and gave us thanks for it in its own fiery way. Sometimes a stone would crack from the heat and startle us and the dogs lying by it. When that happened we would laugh and pretend we had not been startled, of course not, were we not stronger than that? But underneath we all knew we had been and we covered it with laughter.

It occurs to me as I say that I am aware of many times when we covered things with laughter. We sometimes diverted an argument by making fun of one or other of the persons arguing and we would all end up laughing and the argument would be forgotten. You can make someone forget they are in pain if they laugh. We used it as medicine oftentimes. And so, in the noise of which I speak, there was laughter, too.

The endless voices came together to make a solid wall of sound. Everyone talked all the time, to the young, to the newborns, to the elderly and sick on their sleeping platforms for they had to be informed of all that was going on or they would feel neglected.

The noise of many meals being made, of food being prepared, of the mixing of salves and potions for the sick, all had their individual sounds which you could differentiate after a while. The sound of the animals calling for attention or for each other or just because they were bored or a torch had gone out or something. The endless clack of the chickens as they waddled around our feet and our living areas searching for grain which we dropped for them and the calls they made when they laid an egg for us to go and find.

The sound of the footsteps on the cold stone floor endlessly walking to the water source and back again and I do mean endlessly. There was never enough water at any moment for all the needs we had for it.

The sound of knives or sharp stones cutting through hides as we cut and stitched and prepared clothes for ourselves, covers for our sleeping, the sound of knives and stones cutting and chiselling at wood as furniture was made, bowls were carved, toys were carved.

All this noise was echoed back by the stone cold walls of our caves. Every moment of our waking day was a solid wall of noise as impregnable as the barrier.

At night the sounds were there but different; the fire continued to speak even if we were not listening, the animals shifted and complained, the dogs sighed in their sleep. The old and sick murmured as their pains overtook them. Newborns cried in discomfort and were hushed and held by their mothers. Some people would cry out in their sleep and we would make the sigil against the evil one for fear their dreams had been invaded. Sleeping platforms would creak as people tossed and turned. I have laid awake many nights listening to the sounds and been oddly comforted by them, for it meant we were one, we all felt the same, cried the same, slept the same and feared the same.

Smells. Oh my dear channel, how do I describe the smells? Curing hides, cooking meat, ash, resinous wood burning, hot stones; hot people – I am sure you know what I mean by this... smelly newborns, the unmistakeable smell of the women issuing their blood, the wet fur of the dogs, our wastes and that of the animals who contributed their own smells to the mix. When the barrier was put aside, even for the short time to allow us to go out into the sunshine, the smell would go with us as if it were a separate person and it would be waiting for us when we came back in, too.

I would go and tend to the animals so that I could smell the richness of their fodder and hair and wool. That was preferable at times to the smells in the cave.

But then to offset this were the rich comforting smells of the salves we created with crushed plants and berries, mixed with honey which carried its own summer scent.

I have to say that, like the noise, you grew to accept everything and live with it. There was no other way.

Sights. You became used to seeing movement, endless movement as everyone got on with their lives; so much to do all the time. Rarely was anyone still. There was not much colour, we wore the same clothes, we were all dark haired, but we could find colour – at times the flames were beautiful depending on what the fire was burning. The torches glowed yellow and red, the chickens wore red on their heads. For me the joy of Wake was seeing colour, plants, grasses, trees; the intense blue sky, the sunrise and sunset when everything was painted so vividly with the glory of the Great One. I missed this so much during Sleep.

Being confined had its disadvantages; there were problems sometimes, people would squabble over small things, an egg found in someone's area which someone else coveted, a child wandering where it should not and maybe causing damage, the young ones fighting over toys and space, the older young ones resenting tasks, it happened all the time. Mostly it would go away of its own accord. If it got very serious, there might well be a fist fight, it happened but not very often. The Shaman would let it go on, because sooner or later someone would intervene to stop it and if it came from a close family member or neighbour in the cave, it was better tolerated than if the Shaman had stopped it. Rarely did the Shaman have to intervene.

We were the Clan, we were cave dwellers. We had to survive and we did all we could to make sure that we did.

My channel asks: when it got too much for you, or anyone, was there somewhere you could go to just be alone?

Ky replies:

Yes. There was a small cave set aside for the Shaman when he wanted to go into deep trance. I will get to this ere long. Alongside this small cave was another, almost identical as if it had been created especially to mirror the first one. It was lined with hides and had one large pillow in it. A hide could be pulled down to shut it off from the rest of the caves. That was symbolic but everyone respected it. These caves were a good way from the living areas, it grew quieter even as you left the main area to go there and once there, it was almost total peace. Almost, for there can be no such thing as true peace in a place where so many people lived as one.

Once there, you could allow yourself to drift into trance and forget all that was outside, the noise, the conflicts, the demands, the needs of others and for a time just be yourself, drifting on a dream and a wish that it could last a good long time.

You will note I did not say last forever, for no one could wish themselves away from all they knew, loved and respected for the rest of their lives, no matter how long that might be.

My channel asks: can you tell me about your food, what you cooked, what you ate? Did you make strong drinks for celebration, for example?

Ky replies:

We did make a form of drink. I am not sure what you would call it, but we would pick the fruits of one particular tree and add water and let it mature for a whole Sleep. Then we would crush the fruits and the liquid would be shared out. Some people found it very potent and would get rather silly and we would laugh ourselves into stomach aches and hiccups and things.

Other than that, we drank water. In Sleep we heated this and in Wake we drank it cold and fresh. Sometimes we would drop herbs into the water and flavour it if we felt so inclined but mostly the herbs were used for cooking and for medicines.

You are going to ask how we did this. We wove baskets that would hold water, we carved wooden bowls that held water if they were sealed with resins which we gained from certain trees and wood that we found. We would use everything we could to help us in our lives. Some people were skilled at one task, other people skilled at another. Between them we had bowls and containers; we had all that we could need.

Food, we ate a lot of meat, we had a lot of milk from the animals which we made into a sort of cheese if I can go by the cheeses I see in your shops today. Milk was given to newborns in addition to the mother's milk and to young ones. The rest was used for cooking, to make thick sauces for the meat, so it did not become the same old meal all the time. We did not drink it when we were adults, as you do.

We would mix herbs, berries and milk with chopped up meat which would sit by the fire and cook. This was done early in the day so it could be cooking whilst all other tasks were done. We would chase the chickens to discover where they had laid their eggs; sometimes these were added to the sauce, too. Sometimes we just made egg mixtures for speed, especially if we had a day of sunshine during Sleep and could go outside. We were always anxious to go outside but we knew well we had to eat to fortify ourselves before we went out. The fire would be ringed with containers cooking various meals, all this added to the smells in the cave, but they were pleasant smells. It was an occasion when it would make you think 'I wish I was having that family's meal as it smells better than my own.'

My channel asks: can you tell more me about the animals who lived with you?

Ky replies:

I mentioned that we had dogs with us. They were large shaggy animals; something like the ones you call wolfhounds now, but bigger and with longer fur. That fur was valuable to us for stuffing pillows and lining comfortable slings with which to carry newborns. Additional packing of fur to go with the fur lined hides was often needed if a newborn arrived earlier than it should for the cave was a cold, cold place. So we had dogs who roamed from family to family, taking what food that was offered to them, drinking from containers we put down for the other animals, sleeping by the side of the great communal fire. Grooming them to harvest their fur was just another of the tasks we had during the days and nights before we went to our sleeping platforms. They were a joy, though, not a task as much as a pleasure for the dogs responded with affection to those of us who took the time to comb their fur. We used bone which had been carved to let us do that work.

The dogs were useful when we went out to hunt. They could track and bring down an animal for us to kill and carry back to the caves for cutting up and storing. Their reward would be the parts we could not use. As I told you, we wasted nothing.

We did not train the dogs to hunt. They had no names. They were not 'pets' the way your dogs seem to be. They lived with us, we lived with them; we shared lives. They had no reason to know our names and we had no reason to name them. We shared their lives in that they hunted equally with all who went out, they slept alongside the stones of anyone, not associating themselves with one family. You could say we used them but in turn we gave them life, shelter, warmth and food.

We had cats too; as I said, they were bigger than the ones you have now and were valuable in keeping down vermin which would destroy our hides and our stores of food. Cats took care of themselves and did not always attach themselves to any particular family group. They too slept by the communal fire.

Now I remember an odd thing which I confess has just occurred to me. It is the questions you ask, dear channel, that is prompting my memories. I said the stones around the fire were the property of individual families. It was where they heated water and cooked food and none touched anything that belonged to anyone else. Meat would be placed on the stones to cook. I am asking myself now, why did none of these animals ever reach out and take any of that meat for themselves? They were often lying right by the side of the stones; it would have taken but a moment to do that. Of a surety the cats would have wanted the meat cut up for them as they have smaller mouths but the dogs; they could have eaten it without a problem. But they never did. They waited to be fed.

I have to question whether this was the result of the whole atmosphere of the Clan in the cave, the overwhelming respect for one another and their property. Did this affect the animals that lived so closely with us, too?

I think this was so. I think they learned from us as we learned from them, for our lives were closely entwined. You are just now discovering how intelligent your dogs and cats are, we knew that during our time. You lost that information somewhere between our time and yours.

The other animals, the ones we kept in the caves, you will want to know about them, too. We had what you call sheep, what we called sharplans. They grew the woolly coats which we harvested by combing or collecting from briars and thorns generally. It was easy to do. When we left the caves, we carried baskets with lids and bags which closed. Pick up a piece of wool here, a twig or something there, by the time we had completed whatever task had taken us out into the wider world, we would come back loaded with all sorts, from moss to wood and wool. The sharplans were not sheared, as you do, and their wool did not grow as thick. They gave us milk and young ones and wool which we garnered but did not shear to the skin to retrieve. That would have been to disrespect the animal. We kept many of them in the caves all Sleep and left them to graze all Wake. We had dried grasses and other foods for them during Sleep.

We had pigs. Yes, the same name you give them. These are easy to keep in the caves, they ate anything and everything we gave them; leftover food disappeared into seemingly everlastingly empty stomachs.

We had a few cows and a bull. We did not name them; you name yours for some reason. The cows gave us milk, that which the calves did not take, they gave us meat and hides, hooves and hair. Everything was used.

We did not have what you call horses. We saw animals which resembled horses sometimes out in the wild but they ran from us and we did not hunt them or try to bring them into our lives. They seemed strange animals with their long heads and flowing hair on their bodies and tail. Now I see that you ride these animals using a complicated set of straps and buckles to fit round that long head and through that flowing hair which went down their backs. They would have been of use to us but we knew not of that ability and we did not try to work it out. Truthfully, we had enough to do.

So all Sleep we cared for sharplans and pigs and cows and chickens. The chickens roamed the caves, clucking and scratching at the ground and pecking up all sorts of food. We believe they kept us free from lice and other things for they ate anything that moved. They gave us eggs; all we had to do was find them.

It was enough for us to do and enough for us to take care of and enough for us to go into Wake with newborns waiting to arrive, newborn sharplans, pigs and chicks, for the chickens went to sit on their eggs just before Wake arrived. I am sure they knew before the Shaman did when Wake was coming. We could almost time it by the actions of the chickens, by the building of the small nests and the endless sitting on the eggs. It seemed that the eggs hatched about the time we had the celebratory burning of the barrier.

Truly the animals knew more than we did and you would do well to remember that in your modern age.

My channel asks: can you give me an outline of a typical day?

Ky replies:

Let me try. Let me pick a day in Sleep to start. I would be huddled under my heavy hides, with mittens, socks and hood on against the cold. I would wake slowly from a deep sleep when the Shaman began his morning call, banging his stick on the ground. It echoed around the caves. I would hear muttering and murmuring and the creaking of sleeping platforms as people woke and got up.

Our first task was to attend to ourselves, our overnight needs. Then the division of labour would show. Some would immediately rebuild the fire, some would start the fetching of water for everyone and the animals; some would tend to the sick and elderly, helping them with their overnight needs. No one was ever embarrassed at having this help or doing this work, it was something we as a Clan just did. If we found someone who had not survived the night, the Elder men would come and quietly take the body away, as I described to you. This was not an everyday thing, but it happened fairly regularly; we were of all ages, all years and the elderly oftentimes did not survive the cold of the Sleep nights.

If we did not have that sad happening, it was work as usual. Fresh feed was strewn for the animals, grain for the chickens and the young ones would start a hunt for the eggs laid late the day before. These would be used to break our fast, if we found enough. Otherwise we made rough dough and baked it on the stones around the fire. And we began the heating of water and cooking of food for the start of our working day. I would attend to the needs of the Shaman, making sure he had warm drinks and plenty of food. We needed our leader.

When we were gathered round the fire, eating and drinking, there would come a moment – again with no signal – when we would all stop and bow our heads, offering our thanks to the great spirit of the cave for having protected us all night.

Then, again with no signal, we would resume our talking, eating and drinking and then work on.

The floor of the cave needed attention, hides would be taken up, shaken, the floor roughly swept toward the fire, where the rubbish would be scooped up and thrown into the flames. More rubbish would be brought to the fire, used moss, left-over food – a rarity but it happened, if it was not fit for the pigs, it was burned, anything we no longer needed.

If the day was bright and clear, we would venture outside for fresh air, exercise, a restocking of firewood and gathering of any berries left on the bushes.

To do this we would ease aside the barrier just enough for two people side by side to walk through. That left enough space for a person to bring an armful of firewood back into the cave without losing any. It also meant it wasn't too cold in the cave, the fire would be burning steadily and the heat would still build.

Water was thrown down the side of the hill to clear away our wastes; that was done no matter the weather unless the snow was so bad we dared not open the barrier. Those who went outside would take a moment to acknowledge and revere the many spirits around us, the spirits who ruled our lives. I will speak of them later.

By then it would be time for more warm drinks. The animals would need more water; their pens would need clearing out of dung, old straw and uneaten fodder. This occupied quite a lot of the day for those whose task it was to be animal tenders, as this was the time when we milked them for our young ones and elderly. If there was any left, the rest of us would have some, too. We would eat the dough we had left cooking by the fire and then settle down around the stones for warmth and resume our other tasks, carving toys, bowls and other items, stitching new clothing, constructing new sleeping platforms, making all the items we needed to get through our lives. It is then we would groom the dogs and take surplus wool from the sharplans which we would use in many ways to make life more comfortable. There was an endless need for hairs from the animals' tails to make brushes and torches, so every visit to the pens to ensure they were fed and watered and not killing one another would mean a chance to bring back a handful of precious hair. We tried not to waste any journey around the caves. There was enough walking to do to fetch the water.

Some time during the day someone would slaughter one of the animals. Meat was always needed, bone, sinew and hide likewise. It was an endless round of work. I have to say by the time Wake came our herds would be down by about half. The remaining ones would be breeding the next generation for us, in time to be released into the wide world when Wake came.

By sharing everything, we survived. You do not share enough; you are selfish people who tend to shut yourselves away in your homes, not seeing anyone, not talking with anyone, not sharing with anyone. You lock your doors and keep everyone out. You have lost the ability to live in a group. Some of you may think this is a good thing, maybe it is but from our perspective it is bad, we lived close and we survived by caring for one another.

The afternoon, as you call it, would be spent in this way, in between tending to the sick and elderly, getting them up and walking them about if they were capable of walking, keeping the young ones occupied and busy so that they did not get up to mischief and destroy anything that might be of use, in fetching more water – the need for water was endless – and then preparing the meal for the evening. Throughout all this time torches needed making and replacing as they burned out and if there was wall painting going on, we found time to go and contribute to that, too.

After we tidied away from all we had been doing, sewing, carving, woodwork, eating, and the young ones were settled down in their sleeping cradles, we sat and talked, or we had storytelling or trance. What we needed was sleep and that time came soon enough. Sometimes not soon enough, I saw people fall to sleep by the fireside many, many times.

During Wake the work was endless but a little different. We were all but living outside in the sunshine and soft air; we had to watch our animals so that they did not stray too far from our caves and watch for our enemies, too. We took it in turns to keep the fire going in the caves, or the walls would get so cold we would not be able to live in them come Sleep. We searched far and wide for the herbs, berries, honey and firewood we needed, together with fodder for the animals, moss of all kinds to store in case we could not grow enough – even dry moss was useful for the newborns. We collected, we stacked, we stored; we dragged home huge fallen trees and cut them up with our handmade tools – which we added to when we found flint or obsidian or anything strong enough to cut other things.

We went on hunts and added to our meat store and had different hides to work with before Sleep. Everyone needed new clothes. We were hard on our clothes, wearing them day and night as we did and for all the tasks we had, too. During Wake we had ceremonies for the newly bonded, for the newborns who had arrived, for the glory and reverence of the many spirits who governed our world. It seemed we were never without a reason to celebrate something. And of course we had to dig graves for those who did not wake during Sleep and those who did not wake during Wake too. It happened. Often. We did not live long years as you do.

The work was endless but during Wake it seemed lighter for we were outside and there was space between us. It revived us for the time when Sleep came upon us again.

An endless cycle, Wake/Sleep/work. But we did it and we survived, did we not? I now see you are finding Cro-Magnon caves in many places. We did not call ourselves anything but the Clan; the rest is your name to place us in your history. We were survivors, we are your ancestors; we were innovative enough to make use of so much and that enabled us to continue our lives for many cycles of Wake/Sleep. I ask, given your soft way of life, could you do the same?

My channel asks, what did you do for entertainment? By that I mean, did you make music or sing at any of your celebrations?

Ky replies:

We had no musical instruments other than the drum the Shaman would beat to call people to a storytelling or trance session. Music, as you know it and as I like to hear when we work together, was unknown to us. I would say that our days were too full to allow us time to invent any kind of instrument to make music. Our entertainment was the storytelling sessions which we all loved. No one ever missed the call to stories, no matter how sick or wounded they might be. We would carry those incapable of walking so they could be there and take

67

part in what went on, could benefit from a time of not thinking about how ill they were. It was as entertaining for us as your television is for you.

For our celebrations, for the bonding ceremonies, we had special chants which gave thanks to the spirits which surrounded us. We would chant our thanks for the gifts we had, the future personified in another pair bonding, all part of our future.

My channel asks: your days were so long and so full, how did young ones find time to be together, to start the bonding process, to know they were right for one another?

Ky replies:

There is always a way! The walk to the water source was long and wearisome because of the times we had to do it. Walk with someone you want to have in your life and it becomes less of a problem and more of a pleasure. There were the times when we were out in the fields around the caves tending the animals. The girls would pick herbs and flowers, seek out the roots that we could eat and the boys would be tending the animals and helping to search – during Sleep there were times, they would sit together for storytelling or trance, during the evening talk time and again, fetching water. Animals needed tending all the time; it was a simple thing to slip away on the pretext of feeding the pigs with left-over food from the family meal. The caves were not so big that you could not see someone leaving for one of the other caves and yet big enough that it never seemed obvious, until someone pointed it out. Mostly we were consumed with our need for survival, too busy to worry about looking for the bonding going on but when we knew it was there, it was an occasion for joy. We loved to know people were happy together.

My channel asks, you mentioned enemies, who were they and where did they come from?

Ky replies:

I would not have you think we fought pitched battles with other Clans. That was not what I wanted to indicate, more that we had problems with other Clans who tried at times to steal our animals and sometimes even our young. We had to set people to watch every day that we were living through Wake, for fear of losing our supply of meat for Sleep and for fear of losing our young ones. We know at least two were taken, some men heard their cries and ran after them but one was killed with a bone knife and the other was hurt with a large stone and they got away. After that we kept a close watch, as you can understand.

We knew not where these other people came from. They looked like us, had language like us, from what we heard of their shouts and yells, but how far away they lived or why they needed to steal from others was something we never found out. It was just another level of worry in our drive to physically survive the life we had been given to live. On consideration, both the young who were taken were males, so they, these other people, needed males for their future existence. We had to accept by that fact our young were not going to be killed but taken to live full lives somewhere else. Their parents were devastated but there was nothing that could be done. A life had been lost in trying to stop them and another damaged, for the other man was never the same again. The rock hit him on the head.

So we referred to all others, outside our Clan, as enemies. It seemed the right thing to do.

The young who were lost? Their names were engraved on our hearts forever.

Chapter 5 - Shaman

You have not asked, dear channel, but I think the time has come when I must speak of the Shaman to you and those who will read this book. It seems to fit in here quite naturally, so let us go through this important part of our story.

The Shaman was the head of the Clan. It was as simple as that. Everyone deferred to him, his decisions were final. The Shaman was appointed by the Elder Men and Elder Women who considered his past history with the Clan, his predictions, his ability to go into trance and contact those from other worlds to give us our wisdom and advice and help when we needed it. These abilities are not given to many. I was studying with him, even though he was my father he said he saw the abilities in me and I would be a good Shaman in the future.

We had the largest living area in the caves, although we were only two. In truth, we needed the space because of the amount of medicines we made. To do that we needed plants and honey, needed bowls to grind down the plants and mix them with honey to make salves, to mix them with water to make medicines. All this needed space, along with the bowls and containers for all that we made. Was there a day when we were not working from early morning call to final sleep? I do not think so. I carried water, cooked food, groomed animals, helped with sewing, whilst working with the Shaman to make the medicines for the Clan. There were many who were ill or hurt or just needed something to help them get through the days if they were not fully fit.

We kept our few items of clothes in our space but the Shaman's sacred robes were different and needed to be kept very safe. There was a small cave where the Shaman's sacred robes were stored, wrapped in hides with herbs in them so vermin and other creatures could not and would not attack them.

The ceremonial robes were made of the finest, thinnest hides, changed by leaving them in the sunshine. Sometimes they were folded and left to fade, so the hides had lines in them, sometimes they were watered so the sun made its pattern in the drying. These robes were stitched by the older women of our Clan, shut away in a cave kept for that use alone, a small cave with a low roof, painted walls and many totems given by shamans over many years hanging from spurs of rock. They worked with few torches and always in silence. They hurt their eyes and considered it a sacrifice worth making for the robes made the Shaman who made the Clan one people.

This is not to say Leron, my father, could not have chanted and travelled and gone into trance without robes. Of course he could. But with them he was more than just a shaman, he was the Shaman. Just as your priests don robes for their ceremonies before standing before their altars, so the Shaman needed his robes to make him more than himself, to bring us that which we needed.

When a Shaman died and crossed into the afterlife, as part of our mourning we would burn his robes. The women would decide amongst themselves who would prepare the next ones when the new Shaman was chosen. It was a waiting time, a nervous time, for we would be without our leader and who knew what spirit would take advantage of our lack of guidance.

It took a long time to create the robes. The Shaman knew this and respected them. They were kept safe, wrapped in more hides, layered with herbs for their preservation, until needed. When the Shaman walked, bones and teeth clattered from the cords around his neck and woven into his hair and beard, the smell of the herbs went with him as if he was surrounded by a cloud. This was the rich, earthy, almost physical smell of the spirit of nature, the one we revered the most. Without this spirit we would starve.

I may talk more on this, it will come naturally from the questions my channel asks.

My channel asks: Was it only the Shaman who spoke with the spirits or did others have the gift of this, too?

Ky replies:

The Shaman spoke with the spirits of the departed as well as the spirit of the cave, the spirit of nature, the spirit of animals; the spirit of trees. I know some others could hear and see spirit too but they rarely spoke of it, for it would have taken from the Shaman's reputation to be seen doing the same thing. We were sensitive of his standing in the community. Sometimes someone would come with a prediction which was always listened to with great courtesy and followed, if the person was of good standing and not given to hysteria, no matter what it was.

There were those gifted enough to take part in the spirit dances and assist in ceremonies. Mostly these were the Elder Men, those who had been recognised as such. They were also given robes but nothing as finely wrought as the Shaman's. Still they had their own and this set them apart in some way that seemed to please them and was good for the spirits too, for they would sometimes use these Elder Men to give prophesies.

I had my own way of hearing spirit, one my father recognised and acknowledged, but he told no one else of it. I could hear the language of the water.

Where the great river ran through the mountain, it had to go over rocks and down into pools and then on again. We had a place where we could go and collect the ice cold fresh water for the community. That place had many rocks which we used to balance the containers so they would fill with water.

Once everyone had left, I would stay there and listen to the sound of the water as it rushed over the rocks. It had its own voice. Not once did it remain the same, not once did the sound be the same as it was before. Not once did I go there and the voice say the same thing.

It took a long time for me to learn to understand the words of the water. Always it was just out of my reach, like words you want to say but had forgotten, you searched for them and could not find them. The words of the water were like that, a complete language of its own which I had to learn for there was none to translate it for me.

Or that is what I thought.

For a very long time I would listen to the water, trying to say the sounds it made. One time as I sat there, deep in meditation, the sound of the water going through me, I became aware of a spirit presence by my side. The spirit sat down, looked into the water and smiled at me. I recognised the person, it was an Elder, a lady who had passed into the afterlife when I was much younger, when I could walk and talk but not be of help in the community. I remembered her with affection for she was kind with someone who was an outsider, the Shaman's daughter without a mother. It made me different.

She sat with me and by mind to mind contact she told me the language of the water. As soon as she told me, it all became clear and I could hear it myself.

You are going to ask, dear channel, what the water could say.

It spoke of age, of immense age, of the cycle of rain into river into earth and into great lakes.

It spoke of those who took from it, people, animals, creatures not of this earth we would not recognise.

It spoke of those who gave to it, sacrifices, people and goods.

It spoke of those who revered it, those who understood its great wealth of knowledge and our total dependence on it.

It spoke of what it heard, what it saw, what it understood. It might rush by so fast it could not be seen to be going but it saw as it went and it heard as it went and it told me of what was to come.

Of this I will speak at the right time.

Just remember when you are close to water that it understands your words. All of them.

My channel understands this well. She has come close to understanding the language of the water already and she has only just realised it can speak, it does speak, it has the ability to speak. She has realised this and also that she has the ability to understand the language being spoken.

I have spoken with my channel about the water she heard. It is trapped water; it endlessly recycles itself through the noisy thing she says is a pump. Even though it is trapped, the water has its message, for it listens to the birds, the frogs, the fish and the cats which live near it, around it and who drink from it. All is absorbed, all is understood; all is spoken of to those who can hear. Those who can understand.

My channel also knows now that fire, wind, trees and seas have their voice too. She is listening for them.

My channel asks; what did you do when there was a serious dispute which could not be resolved by the Shaman? It must have happened.

Ky replies:

You are right. At times a dispute grew serious enough that even with the Shaman's intervention it could not be resolved. I have to say that it was usually a person trying to steal another's hand-fasted partner. Theft was rare, we had so little anyway. I recall one time there was a murder. That shocked the whole Clan for a very long time.

When anything serious happened that could not be sorted out, that person was ostracised immediately and permanently. It is not possible to live within a group where no one speaks to you, helps you, allows you space at the fire or includes you in the storytime evenings. You can spend just so long crushed against a wet wall, lost, alone. That person always, always walked out of the cave and never came back.

Their names were carved in our hearts, with immense sadness.

My channel asks: tell me about your father's trance sessions and storytelling sessions, for I imagine they were quite different.

Ky replies:

Yes, they were. Let me start with the trance sessions.

We never knew when the times would be. I don't think my beloved father knew when they would be. At the end of the day he would sometimes strike the drum in a slow, almost mournful way and we would come, walking quietly into the big cave, each carrying our stick and a roll of hide. Please note I said 'our' stick. Everyone had one. It was something they had found and carved for themselves; it was the perfect size to walk with, to use as a weapon, to use as we did in trance sessions, to make the sound that helped the Shaman travel.

It seemed a very short time before the entire Clan was sitting in a big circle around the fire. Each person unrolled a hide and put it on the cold floor. Each was bigger than the person needed, so everyone had a portion of another hide to sit on. The children were nearest the fire and had their own small sticks and hides.

The Shaman was on a raised platform, higher than the ones we used for sleeping, so that he was above us and we could all see him. He wore his sacred robes and sometimes held a special herb in one hand which he rubbed and then smelled his fingers. The oil, the essence of the herb, was what he needed sometimes. He would not acknowledge us but put his drum to one side and sat back, waiting.

As if at a signal - but I never saw one given, we all began banging our sticks on the floor in perfect unison. Even pounding the sticks on hides, the noise was incredible. The sound would echo around the cave, the bats would rustle and squeak and sometimes take off, a whole flight of them pouring out of the cave, leaving us to the spirit world. The rhythmic sound would go on and then just as suddenly stop as we saw the Shaman's head begin to fall forward, eyes rolled back in his head, lips stretched over his teeth. There was something strange about the way he looked at that time, as if he was not of this earth. His skin would take on a different hue; there would be a wild strange look in his sightless eyes. I knew well he saw nothing at that time for he told me this when we were having lessons on all he knew.

Then we would be silent, utterly silent. I never understood how the small ones could be so still, no whining, no crying; no complaining. It was as if the spirit of the cave cast a spell over everyone so that we were silent and still. I think of the age of some of the elders and knew that sitting so still would cause problems with joints when they tried to rise and yet they too did not move.

And then, quietly, the Shaman would begin to speak. Sometimes he would begin in a language we did not understand and yet... I say this and I believe we did understand on a deep, deep level, beyond any of our comprehension. Because the words resonated in some way. Then he would speak our language and talk to us of stories told by the other world people and we knew then that the stories came direct through the Shaman from the other world people and we would be in awe of his ability to connect with them and for them to use him to speak to us.

Sometimes he would tell us of a way to make life easier, that if we did this or that, our daily work would be better. He told us once of a better way to make containers, to line them and coat them so they did not leak water when brought from the spring. He told us how to cleanse the hides so they lost their smell. He told us how to make the fire burn endlessly without a lot of work by putting the wood just so and not the way we had it, stacked high in the centre of the circle. He told us of many things which when we thought about it, were obvious but we were so concerned with our day to day living, with preparing for the next season, that we had little time in which to experiment and to think on it for a moment.

To experiment with the great fire was dangerous, for if it went out it would be a long and cold period before we could light it again. So he told us about banking up the ashes to make a barrier against the falling out of the wood and how to take some of the ash away and use it to cleanse the area we used for wastes, how to sprinkle it in the caves for the animals to stand on, to make a deep thick covering for them to ease their hooves, how to use it to clean bowls and other things for it would scrape at the insides and cleanse them. How we could clean our obsidian knives and weapons by using shallow containers of ash, immersing the blade in them and rubbing hard with pieces of hide or bark. We used ash as much as we used the animal skins themselves to make every part of our life a little better. The fire was the central part of our lives, it kept us warm, it cooked our food; it preserved our hides and gave us both light and ash to use as well. Could anyone ask for more than that? And yet it was more than that, the voice of the fire was comforting and friendly, it whiled away many a long dark night while we waited for the light to come so we could start another day. It greeted us if we had been outside and had grown cold; it awaited us on warm Wake days when the cave was lit with its flickering endless flames which matched the sun rays which reached us. Like the water we took from the ever flowing river, the fire was ever burning and ever there and ever essential to our lives.

I divert but I divert to tell you that which you needed to know: how essential the great fire was in our lives.

The Shaman would talk of our spiritual being, of the way we had to look at the world outside and the world inside the cave, how to study the cracks and fissures in the cave walls and use them, where we could grow more moss, where we could collect finely filtered water which had come from the great outside through the cracks and into our lives. This water was held to be sacred and precious and we gathered it with reverence. He told us how we could use the fissures to hold our belongings if we did not want them on the cave floor. Such small things but to us such big things.

He would tell us of the great worlds beyond the stars which we saw each night the cloud did not come and hide us from their eyes. Worlds of flaming storms and tempests, worlds of rain and endless winters, worlds of beings we could not begin to understand with our human minds but which we would try and paint when a wall revealed itself as needing our decoration.

And he would end with a small story that would hold us even more still.

I want to say here that when he beat the drum and we gathered round the fire, flames leaping to the roof, bats rustling and murmuring to themselves, they too would be silent and listen, when the bodies stopped moving and the hides stopped sliding against one another, the sense of anticipation was so great I could almost feel the breath stop in my mouth.

Then he was not my loved father but the serious revered knowledgeable leader, the one all deferred to and I would feel sick to my stomach at the thought that one day we would bind his body in hides and lay him in the death cave.

Foolish Ky; I did this every time we gathered for stories.

But I must not dwell on these things. I want to tell of this time of the great stories we were given. This one came from a time before our time. We were told stories like these by others, older than us, wiser than us and from worlds other than ours. We were told them so that we could pass them on to those who would hear.

This one he said was a story about a great flood.

And so it was that for some reason the spirit of the wind and the spirit of the snow and rain argued. Some say it was caused by their love for the spirit of nature and she refused to choose either one but said she would stay as she was, of her own self and because of this the two spirits fought one another as only they could.

And the spirit of the wind brought storms and vast scary ferocious winds to batter the earth, to tear up the trees, to damage the mountains, to try and get into the caves where the people lived.

And so the people cowered in our caves and were afraid to go outside for fear of being blown down the side of the mountain and lost forever and so the people waited for the ferocious winds to stop.

And they did. Suddenly. No dying away, no easing, no warning, just there and then not there.

And then the spirit of the snow and rain began his side of the battle. The snow fell in huge amounts, building up, covering everything until even the tops of the trees were gone from sight. And the people were afraid they would never be able to leave the caves again for there were no pathways, no woods; no way to know where they were going. The wild animals were silenced, the land silent for the snow made no sound as it fell. Not even a whisper as it landed.

And they waited and waited and then one day they heard the sound of water running. The snow was melting.

And it took a long, long time to melt. There was so much snow that when it melted it made a flood that covered all the land. It looked like the great seas we had been shown, so vast was the land covered by water.

And the people worried that the animals, wild and ones they had not gathered in, had been lost in the flood but they had climbed to a high mountain to escape the snow as best they could and so they survived.

And the land was damaged by the water which took a long, long time to go away. The nature spirit was not pleased with the spirit of the wind or the spirit of snow and rain, for they had damaged her world and it took a lot of work to make it right again.

In the end neither of them won her love.

And the animals came down from the mountain and began their lives again as best they could.

And the spirits of the wind and the snow and rain vowed never again to fight one another but to serve the people in every way they could.

The shaman said that when the strangers came to talk to the people of this great flood, they found out that the people did not know what seas were. So the strangers gave the people pictures, mind to mind, of vast areas of water which rippled gently and flowed to the land and then sometimes rose up in huge amounts and crashed down on the land and took some of it away. And the people were afraid of the water and said they would never go near such a place.

Then he would stir, his eyes would close and then open again and he would smile and we would bang our sticks in joyous recognition and acceptance of the great gift he had just given us – his mind, his heart and his connection with other world people.

Then someone would help him rise from his platform and we would gather up the small ones and assist the elders and we would all return to our part of the caves with new wisdom and a new story to think on as we slid into the darkness of sleep for another night.

These were very special nights, full of drama and information, of wisdom and of companionship. Listening together as we did, being taught as one as we were, bound the Clan even more tightly together. It is this which made the outcast, when that happened, even more sorrowful for them and for us.

The storytelling sessions were lighter, often full of laughter and chants that sometimes we did not know we knew. If you can understand this?

The drum beat for this was different and everyone came in a rush, for storytelling times were special, were looked forward to with great anticipation. They lifted our hearts and minds for ours was an endless fight just to survive. We had none of your labour saving ways and knowledge; we were battling all the time. Any relief from the battle was welcome.

Again we brought our hides and our sticks and we sat around the fire. This time the Shaman would not be on a high chair above us, but part of us, sitting with us around the fire. Once we had all settled, he would look at all of us and start:

"There was a time…" All the stories started this way. Magical words that drew us in immediately. I can remember holding my breath when the stories began, only releasing it when I felt a pain in my chest.

It was at these times we would hear the stories of the giants, the huge men who could cover much ground with one stride. Terrifying creatures that carried huge clubs to break down trees as if they were twigs, able to bestride rivers and who would not have been afraid of the waters of the seas as we were.

We heard of animals with single horns on their heads, delicate animals that walked as a deer would but lightly, hardly leaving a cloven hoof mark on the ground to show their passing. It was said their coats shone like the summer sun at all times, like silver in the light of the moon, like – I have run out of words to tell you how their coat would shine so different from all other animals. These I would wish I could see for myself, for they sounded beautiful and I did so love everything beautiful, whether it was the flower on a herb or The One covering the sky in reds, pinks and other colours at dark when the stars were ready to come out and watch over us.

We heard of the bird which rose from its own ashes, with huge sweeping wings that would cover a huge distance if held out and feathers that could be used to ride on were we able to harness the great winds that blew across our land.

We heard of great creatures which roared flames from their mouths; had great wings that beat the air and let them fly and of people, not our people, who rode on their backs and covered huge distances, far more than we could walk in a lifetime of walking. It was said these things lived in their own realms and we were grateful that they did for could we live with such things our lives? Things which would send flames to char us to death?

We heard of men with horse bodies or horses with men instead of heads and necks. The Shaman never said which was which and we did not ask, for we could not comprehend such a creature and were content to know that it lived on another world and would not come to us.

We heard of the monsters called Minotaurs and I have to say the same thing…

We heard of what other people called Gods, those who lived on high mountains and had hammers that made the thunder and threw light to make the lightning which so scared our animals and made us run for shelter when it happened. I know, from your many books, that these Gods supposedly lived in great halls and in great splendour and many of your people believe in them. We did not have to believe in them, for they were no part of our lives. We had our spirits and our protection and it was enough for us to listen to the stories and go to our beds grateful we had nothing to worry about from them.

The stories were good, even if it meant that we were often woken from sleep by young ones crying out from bad dreams. The stories did tend to linger in the mind. We would hear the mother hushing the young one, saying it was just a dream, just a story and they would slide back into the darkness of sleep, content knowing they were safe. Dreams were often used for prophesy but we would be careful not to listen to any dream dreamed after a night of storytelling.

I knew well that the Shaman spoke with the other world people in his sleep and in his quiet times, when he shut himself away in a tiny cave just big enough for him to crawl into and be alone. I must tell you of those times.

He had a hide which hung down from jutting out knobs of rock above the opening, as if made for such a thing. One of the Elder Women tied sinews to the corners of the hide and in turn these were tied to the jutting out knobs. When the Shaman needed to be alone, he would take his carved stick, go to this tiny cave, crawl in and lower the hide. Then none went near him. He had furnished it, with my help, with thick pillows of straw stuffed into hides so he would have some comfort and he would wrap himself in wool from the sharplans. There was a lot of it in the cave. So he would be almost in a cocoon just as the caterpillar did before turning into a graceful butterfly. This was how I saw my beloved father, a caterpillar, waiting for the day when he would return to the spirit world and be a butterfly.

There he would stay for maybe two days, maybe more. He would emerge needing water, food and proper sleep. I would be aware of his awakening, somehow we were connected, and I would rush to the cave and attend to him. He would lean on me as we went back to our living area and let him fall down onto his sleeping place. Then I would return to his cave, take away the containers of his wastes, attend to the pillows and hides and make it clean and tidy again ready for the next time.

By the time I returned to my father, he would be asleep. I would prepare food and have cold fresh water waiting for him when he woke. Only then would he tell me what he had learned on that journey. Later he would share it with the Clan at a different kind of meeting.

It is hard to describe things which we were so used to, my channel! We knew the difference between the meetings but I need to tell you about it and I need to think how to say it.

When my father had been in trance for as much as two days or more, he would be very tired when he came back to our world, not quite right, dizzy and weak. So he would need days of rest, of food and a lot of clear fresh water which I would bring for him, not the stale water which we got in the morning and which was sometimes still there at dark. He needed the fresh water, full of the chattering of the water spirit's voice. When he was strong again, he would make a different rhythm with the drum and all would gather around the fire to hear the words from the other world where he had been.

I have to say there was an eagerness for all such occasions. Without them our lives were a routine of work and more work, so much to do all the hours of daylight, preparing for the next period, whether it be Sleep or Wake. Animals needed tending no matter the time period, so did the sick and elderly and those carrying the newborn. The caves needed attention, cleaning and tidying and then painting. But first let me talk of these trance meetings, if I can call them that.

There was an air of anticipation when we gathered to hear the results of a trance by the Shaman. It was different from being there when the Shaman went into trance, for we were able to ask questions, to say 'how wonderful!' or something like that as he talked. We knew he liked it for his face would light up when something was said. It was acknowledgement of his skill, his ability to communicate with the other world people. We were not demonstrative people, we did not hug and kiss and hold hands and take one another's arms as I see you do in your time. We would hold the arm of an aged one or a little one trying to walk, we would help a sick one sit up to take food or drink but in everything else, we maintained our distance. It was no more than a reaction to being closed in the caves for so long, it was better to avoid contact for fear of causing offence and causing a problem. So, no one would approach the Shaman, shake his hand and say 'well done, Leron!' for that was not our way. Someone would call out from the gathered Clan something like 'wonderful, Leron!' or "tell us more, Shaman!' and he would respond with his gentle smile which never changed and he would continue with his recital.

His journeys were so involved, so incredible it was hard to think one person could experience so much. The worlds where he went were entirely different from ours, worlds where there were more than one sun and several moons, where light was ever present, where the people had to make darkness to rest. There were worlds where there was no light from the skies and the people had to make light to see and go about their lives. We could understand that, for the long days of Sleep often meant we lived with torches and used the fire itself to light our lives and let us get busy with our many tasks. We could not sleep the entire time away, there was too much to do to get ready for Wake.

So we welcomed these trance meetings, we could shout our encouragement to our Shaman, we would learn of things which were strange and beyond our understanding and yet, and yet we knew them to be true, somewhere inside ourselves. We would be enriched by these meetings as much as we were enriched by the other trance evenings and storytelling evenings. We had variety and interest in that way, despite everything we knew we could rely on the Shaman for lifting our spirits.

Yes, life was one long battle for survival. We needed heat, shelter and coverings, we needed food and water. These five things consumed our entire lives. The finding and gaining of them, the dealing with them, the living with them. It is hard, if not impossible, for you to understand how this worked, but I am sure you will understand our need for them all.

My channel asks: did you ever meet any of these people from other worlds? Or did they only speak through the Shaman?

Ky replies:

I have wondered if you would ask this question – wondered whether it would come into your mind that not all our wisdom and advice came through the Shaman to us. I also wondered at length whether to tell you the truth. It would be easy to say of course we did not, we were nothing but cave dwellers and we lived a simple life, learning what we could from the Shaman who used trance to contact these people.

But you know, dear channel, that in truth that would not be true. You know of the cave paintings of 'aliens' as you call them, drawings of the vehicles they used to come to us and drawings of how some of them looked.

Yes, we met people – strange beings – from other worlds. They came to us as we were receptive. We were not judgemental. We spoke with them with our minds and they answered us in the same way. We did not speak aloud with them for they had no ears. This they mimed to us.

In our time of Sleep, we would become aware of different beings in the caves. Sometimes we knew that these beings were the spirits of our loved ones who had not survived the night. These we recognised and were pleased to know they were there with us. They watched over us and guarded us and we relied on them for that protection.

Sometimes the beings would be what you call bipedal, two legs, two arms, head, and these we could identify as beings from another world. These were the ones who spoke with us mind to mind and we could ask questions and receive answers. I have to say if we met such people now, we would ask very different questions but then we knew little to nothing of the great universe you now know of, the many galaxies and universes and star clusters. For us the night sky was full of lights, pinpoints of lights which we did not know were clusters, did not know that they were often shadowed by a twin dark star or planet. We just – accepted they were there and that the beings we spoke with came from somewhere in there. Our perceptions were limited by our knowledge. So we asked about our lives, how to make them better. It was they who told us about making needles to sew our clothes, talked to us of drilling the holes in fine strong bone to draw sinews through. They said they knew nothing of our animals but could see the worth of the sinews which we had for we used them for everything, as I have told you. And so we became proficient at making clothes. I wish I could remember the questions, the results, which you would be interested to know but it all became part of life, their visits were part of life, we never questioned them as to why they came, why they wanted the contact. I think now they wanted to see whether we were any threat to them and when they saw we were not, they helped us all they could.

There were others who moved among us, shapeless, sometimes shadows, sometimes blue lights, sometimes yellow and red flickering lights. These we knew were strangers from other worlds but we had no way of speaking with them for we could not receive from them.

Or so we thought. It was only one evening, one end of day meeting – oh I am sorry, dear channel, in my haste to tell you so much I have omitted the end of day meetings! I wanted to talk with you of the storytelling, the trance, the great effect that had on our lives, but overlooked the simple ones.

At the end of a day, we would gather round the fire and talk. We would discuss our problems, maybe an animal was sick, maybe a person was sick, maybe someone was not happy, this was common during Sleep when we were locked in the cave for so long, maybe someone was injured, maybe someone had a new way to season and prepare a meal – all this would be shared with the Clan. We would offer advice, accept advice, listen to ways of making food more interesting, ways to make an animal better and so on. These were informal gatherings, not everyone came. Sometimes people left half-way through to go to their sleeping platforms, being overcome by tiredness, for we lived busy physical tiring lives, as I have said. Sometimes we sat late by the fire and talked, for we started on topics that would keep us going for a while. And sometimes we sat late to talk for companionship; a sleeping platform can be a lonely place with none to share it with you.

It was during some of these gatherings that we would realise the stranger beings had spoken with us for someone would say something profound that we had not thought of, or considered, before. It would be said in a way that was stilted sometimes, unlike our usual free-flowing language. It would be said as if it had come from another Clan, another group. It was then we realised we were receiving and we were sorry we could not and had not responded. Then the Shaman told us, after one of his trance sessions, that they did not mind we had not responded, that the fact we had received was reward enough for them. We know they continued to come for we saw them from time to time, maybe a few times during Wake and more regularly during Sleep, for then we were receptive, being all but prisoners in our cave complex.

We welcomed our visitors and were eternally grateful for their immense and tremendous journeying to reach us.

I have just thought of something I did not realise at the time; did these beings take over our people without us knowing? Did they come and live among us, taking on the bodies of the Clan members and that is why they spoke in an odd different way? I will never know now but the thought sits right in my head.

My channel asks: on this subject, did you ever meet with other Clan/cave dwellers? Or were all strangers treated as enemies? How did you know the difference?

Ky replies:

Yes, we did meet with others, not as often as we would like but we had travellers come to the caves and they were welcomed as were the strangers from other worlds. We, our Clan as a whole, did not travel. We stayed where we were, knowing the area around our caves and living within its boundaries. Sometimes the younger ones, newly bonded perhaps, had visions of other places, other Clans and would leave us to go on their journeying. We could not ask them not to go, it was their choice but none ever returned to tell us where they had been and who they had seen and, more important than that, what they had seen.

The difference between our enemies and the visitors is this: the enemies would hide from us, would watch us from afar; would make rushes toward our animals and young ones. Visitors came bold, walking into our area with hands out-stretched and sticks held horizontal and calling a welcome to us. When this happened all work ceased as we gathered to greet them.

We welcomed these visitors and always sought to find out if they had seen or heard of our missing ones. They never had. That we put to one side to mourn over and keen over later. Before then we had talk to share, what their life was like, whether they did things differently to us so we could learn from them or in turn whether they could learn from us. We were anxious for the end of the day meeting time to come so we could gather round and talk with our visitors. Before then they were good enough to help us with our many tasks: firewood, water collecting, sweeping, cleaning; tending the sick. This was invaluable; I have to say that, the sick were encouraged by strangers coming to talk with them and bring their tidings from another area, another Clan. We noticed that many sick made a dramatic improvement when we had visitors, boredom can play a big part in keeping someone on their sleeping platform.

There was much work to do, finding spaces for our visitors to leave their possessions and to sleep, we sorted out hides and pillows, bowls and extra food for them, we did all we could to make them welcome, hoping they would come again if they were travelling.

After several evenings of talk, the Shaman would go into trance and they too were able to hear the words from the strangers from other worlds. It was then we would discover that the visitors did not have a Shaman as their leader and had no contact with or understanding of other worlds. I recall the time one group left a young man behind when they moved on. The Shaman trained him in the shamanic ways, he had lessons alongside me and when they returned our way a whole Sleep and Wake later, he was able to go with them, fully able to communicate with other worlds. He was the only one I recall having the ability to do this. It made our Clan different, which gave us pride. When visitors came and spoke of our Shaman, our knowledge of other people, which they had learned from those who visited us before, we were proud but tried not to show it. The Shaman would not have been pleased with us had we boasted of what we knew, so we acted as if it was an ordinary thing for us and left them to make up their own minds.

Sometimes I felt they liked our end of day meetings better; then they could share their knowledge and experiences. In the trance evenings they could not, they were at a disadvantage, we knew more than they and it put them back a bit. The Shaman even talked of not going into trance for them, but others said he should now that we were known for it. There was good reasoning on both sides. The final decision was always left to the Shaman; after all he was the one being used.

You see I make the difference between enemies who stole and visitors who shared. Our enemies could have benefited from all we had to offer had they come in friendship, instead of coming to steal. Another sadness we carried with us on our life journeys.

We talked of the visitors who came to us many times after they had moved on. We needed the interest but oh, how much better for us would it have been if they could have told us about our young ones who had left and not come back!

My channel asks: you mentioned painting the walls. Can you tell me about the paintings?

Ky replies:

Painting was an essential part of our lives. No matter how much work we had to do – and as I have told you, there was a lot of work to do – we found time to paint.

First we created the paints, mixing earth, clay, powdered herbs and flowers to make the different colours. Black was easy, we used burnt wood from the fire mixed with thick clay and animal urine which had been stored for that purpose, to make the mixture.

Our brushes were hairs from the animals, usually the tail, which they shed regularly. These were gathered and tightly bound to the end of small sticks. Nothing was wasted in our lives.

The Shaman would start work on a wall; he would create the first outline, perhaps an animal, perhaps a hunter, perhaps a line of mountains and then stand back. Those of us chosen to add to that wall would step forward with small bowls full of colour and add our ideas to the scene. Then the wall would be allowed to dry. This could take some time for as I have said, with so many of us living together, the walls were always running with water from our breathing. When the wall dried, the Shaman would summon others to come and add their ideas to the scene. So it would develop, with different aspects being added and the scene changing all the time. It was a source of wonder to us, we would go and stand and stare at it for a time. It was a break from our work, a chance to think of what we would add next time if we were chosen and to wonder how the Shaman would seal the painting with his special signs and sigils as protection from all that would attack us. The paintings were for our benefit, giving us something to do, something to look at; something to think about but underneath that was the real reason; the paintings were sacred and created for protection from all unseen forces.

We do not know but we reason that the other cave paintings were created for the same reason. There is so much work to do for all of us living in this Before Time era that you speak of, that to take time to make a painting means that it is a highly important if not sacred thing to do. It would be much easier to leave the cave walls as they were, as the spirit of the cave created them. But we always asked for permission to decorate the cave walls and, when we were finished, we felt the warmth of the spirit around us, knowing it was pleased with what we had done.

The people who find cave paintings now miss this part of their existence entirely. They only see the hunts, the people; the rough outlines. They do not see the spiritual protection granted to us cave people by the Shaman's special skills when the picture was completed. They do not see it for they do not understand the spirituality of my people. They never have done. To them we are no more than one step away from creatures that grunt and do not have intellect. I hope this book will prove that to be totally false. I hope that they will be open enough to change their thinking.

I am sad to say I do not think they will.

My channel asks: You have mentioned spirits many times in this narrative so far, can we talk about the individual ones?

Ky replies:

It is essential that we do, for you to understand how close we lived with the spirits of our world.

I am sad to see that you – by this I mean the people of your world – do not care for the spirits which are around them. There are too few people like you, dear channel, who understand the way the spirit world works, who see spirit in all that is around you.

But let me talk of the spirits as I knew them.

The greatest spirit was The One, who had no name, the one who created the world on which we lived, who was responsible for the arc of the sky and the setting of the millions of stars in the darkness, the one who made and set the stars which were not stars, which did not move as stars, the red one, the shining one and who put the golden one in the sky for us to have light and heat and good feelings. This spirit was responsible for all prayers, all chants, all rituals and all activities that we had to help us live.

The others were lesser spirits but only in that they had less work than The One.

We held rituals throughout the year to appease and placate The One, so that he would not turn his face from us, not take the starlight and the golden one from us and leave us in total darkness. We cave-dwellers feared the darkness above all for in the darkness evil beings could find us and attack us, even though we painted the walls and the Shaman signed the sigils for our protection. Evil beings had been known to take newborns and destroy them in some way, for we never found them again. Evil beings had been known to take the senses of some of the older people so they did not know who they were and where they were and we had to be with them all the time for fear of them hurting themselves. This happened in the darkness of Sleep and so we danced and chanted and sacrificed to The

One that he would not turn away from us and cast us into eternal darkness.

We sacrificed animals and burned great fires outside the cave so that The One might see and know we had made the ritual the way he wanted it to be. We laid the best parts of the animal sacrifice on a large stone we had dragged into position and the Shaman had blessed with chants and oils. We left it there and cowered in our caves all night, hearing the heavy footsteps as The One came close, the snarling and chewing as The One ate that which we left for him and the sound of him moving away, bringing relief and peace to our minds and hearts again.

We made our sacrifices and our rituals all through Wake and sometimes, if the weather was good enough, we would light the fire and make the sacrifice and ritual during Sleep, in the hope that the extra ritual would please The One. We were never without the golden ball or the stars, so he must have been satisfied with the offering by his people.

The spirit of the moon was one that was hard to understand. At times it hid its face from us, sometimes it hid part of its face from us; sometimes we saw all of it and sometimes, the really frightening times, it hid itself so completely we could not see anything of its being. We worshipped this spirit for when the moon showed itself, even partly, we could see to walk about outside in the darkness. This moon travelled across the sky each night, as if looking at all we did and had done. It made us aware of what we had to be at all times, polite and kind and helpful to one another.

This spirit also had sacrifices and rituals so that it did not permanently turn its face from us and deny us the night light we sometimes needed. When the spirit turned its face from us, the Shaman would call us all to a fire outside, where we would chant and dance a slow moving dance that took us around and around the fire in one great snake that had eaten its tail. It moved slowly and gently, every person offering their own prayer to the spirit that it would turn its face back to us. Finally a small animal was sacrificed and left on the sacred stone for the spirit to consume. This one was not cooked on the fire; the Shaman declared that this spirit took the blood sacrifice rather than the meat. That, he said, was left for such animals as lived outside the caves that also needed placating so we could walk in safety when we left our home.

I truly loved the spirit of the moon. The silver of the light enchanted me. I saw with such clarity at night when the light was full shining on the ground and all that grew and lived around us. It distressed me when the spirit turned its face from us and my prayers were fervent and heartfelt indeed that it would show itself again. I understood that sometimes it wanted to hide from us behind the clouds but the clear nights when it turned away were troublesome to my mind.

Then there was the spirit of the wind. This spirit spoke in roars during Sleep, battering the caves and sending rocks flying down the sides to scare us as we huddled together in the darkness, wondering what we had done to annoy the spirit. This spirit would throw things at our barrier as if seeking a way in, too. We were all afeared of this spirit when it seemed enraged; we knew not how to placate it. We would stay scared and worried in our cave, hearing the sounds, wondering what would be seen outside when we could leave. When we ventured out after this roaring and shouting we would find much had been broken, much wood that we could carry home for the fires and for this we were grateful, we did not have to cut it ourselves. Trees that were dragged from the earth were towed back and cut up so we only made one journey.

It was a frightening spirit that we would seek to placate if we could only find the way. We tried the usual sacrifice, chants, dances and silent meditation, but it would still throw angry fits and try to pummel the caves and us into submission. The Shaman could not find the answer from the people in other worlds, either; they had no knowledge of this spirit and could not help us.

But then sometimes the spirit spoke in gentler ways, in softer winds that blew away the smells of our bodies and our animals; that brought the smell of flowers and herbs so we knew where to find them. Then we would dance a celebration and chant our thanks to the spirit and hope that it would understand our needs and not be so ferocious in the days to come. During Wake it would be reasonable, during Sleep it was savage, as if it did not wish us to shut ourselves away but we had no other way to ensure our survival through the terrible cold and snow.

The spirit of the snow and rain. Rain we needed to make the grass grow, to make the trees put out their leaves in Wake, to fill the rivers so the earth had its moisture and the animals had their drink. Snow we needed to cover the earth and protect it from the bitter coldness of the middle of Sleep. We needed these spirits and yet we had the problem of rain coming too hard for too long, when the rivers could take no more and spilled water over the sides and into the areas where we had found herbs and plants we needed. We were ever afraid they would be washed away when the water found its way back into the river.

We had the problem of snow piling up against our barrier and if we were not able to keep a passageway through it, we found the smoke would fill the caves and we would be coughing and choking and the bats could not find their way out. The frozen snow did keep the heat in but we needed a small space for the air to go in and out.

Good small levels of snow were what we needed and often we would go out into it, roll in its chill and cleanse ourselves of all that was biting us – at least for a while.

If we knew how to placate the spirit of rain and snow, we would, but we could only do our best and hope that our small sacrifices were enough to at least give us some good rain and good snow and help us endure the too much rain and too much snow when it came.

The spirit of the land was our friend. It was this spirit which made the grass to grow, the rains to fall, the flowers and herbs to grow fully so we could harvest our special plants to make our salves and potions. This spirit encouraged the animals to eat and drink, the animals' young to grow into adults, to protect them from predators both on the earth and in the sky. This spirit encouraged the milk in the animals so there was enough for the young and for us. This spirit caused the birds to lay eggs and the young to grow into adults so that there would be food. Those of us skilled enough with slingshot and stone could bring them down and those skilled with such things would pluck and cleanse the bird and stuff it with herbs and other good things to eat.

We would make sacrifices to this spirit, in love and in gratitude. We would offer to it the finest plants, the prettiest flowers; the tenderest young animal and we would dance slow and long, sometimes into the night, losing ourselves in the dance, to the sound of the pounding of the drum and the beating of the great log with carved sticks. Endless rhythms. The men would take it in turns, overlapping with one another so there would be no break in the sound and no break in our dancing. One by one we would fall down and the others would dance around and over us until every star was out and beaming down its silent light to us. Then and only then would we rise up from the ground and go to our beds.

The spirit of the animals was another important spirit to worship and placate. Our animals were our livelihood in every way. We used them for their milk, their meat, their coats, their hooves and horns and bones and sinews. We used them. We treated them as honoured members of the Clan; we attended to their every need all through Sleep and gave them rich grazing during Wake. We forgave the kicks, bites and pushes; we groomed them and nursed them through illness and birth. We supervised their mating to ensure good offspring. Their deaths were always a sacrifice by us to the spirit of the animals before we made use of any part of them. You go to a shop to buy your meat, pre-packaged and clean and untainted with any natural thing. Your animals are kept shut away, bred for meat and not for themselves. I see the difference and I know the meat does not enrich you for it has nothing of the earth and the air and the wind and the rain in it. The spirit of the animals has long since returned to the Great One as it no longer has work to do. Even those of you who profess to live what you call 'organically' are playing at it. For they were fed and grew on this lifeless meat before they made the decision to go 'organic.' I am sorry if this offends, it is the truth as we see it from our side of life. You have long lost the ways of living close to the earth. Your inability to accept spirit when it is given to you, no matter how it is given to you, shows us that.

You asked last night, dear channel, about the spirit of the caves. You said, from the depths of the darkness when you were supposed to be sleeping, that it was the most important spirit of all to us. You are right. It was.

We worshipped the spirit of the caves. We held it in the highest possible regard. We knew that without this spirit the caves could collapse, could trap us; could destroy us. What kind of sacrifice could we make to placate this spirit? The Shaman talked long on this subject. One of us suggested human sacrifice but the Shaman said no. It was decided after much talk that our sacrifice would continue to be the respect with which we treated the caves. We did not allow anyone to alter anything. One entrance to and from a food cave had a piece of rock sticking out on which we caught our legs time and time again. Sometimes it would cut the skin and the person would be injured. But we could not and would not knock it out and create a clear way through, for that would be to injure the cave and the cave spirit. We made no holes for our torches; we used ones already there even if they were not in the right place. We would not make new holes. Before we painted a wall, we would ask permission of the spirit of the cave to do this. We would wait for two days to see if anyone had an answer. If the Shaman did not receive a reply, someone in the Clan would. The spirit never ignored us. We asked the spirit of the caves for permission before we chose one cave as a place to lay our dead during Sleep. It was the biggest thing we could ask of the spirit, could we store our dead in its heart until such time as we could return them to the ground from which they came. We asked the spirit for permission to light the huge gathering fire and for help to keep it burning. It never went out even when the spirit of the wind and rain sent sharp gusts into the cave during Wake and tried to silence it.

So we venerated and respected the spirit of the caves and in return the spirit held the caves so that we could live in them. What more could the Clan ask?

My channel asks, you mentioned the choosing of a stone for the young women who had a first bleed. I have been wondering if there was a ritual of some kind for the young men who made their first kill during a hunt.

Yes there was. When our young males reached the age at which that which makes them truly male emerges and their voice changes, they are taken by the older experienced men on a hunt. If this is during Sleep, then they wait for a day of sunshine and go out to see if they can add to our food supply. The young male is equipped for the first time with a knife gifted by the Elder Men, one they have worked on during the time of 'rest' when the day's other work is done. If there is more than one young male, more than one Elder Man works on a knife.

They usually attack something relatively small; there is no point in losing our young through over-ambition of a large kill so it is chosen with care and the young male is allowed the final killing cut or stab if you like. Then, as the blood pours from the animal, the Elder Man takes some of it and daubs the young male on the cheeks and forehead. With this mark clearly displayed, they return to the cave, bringing their kill with them. There is additional feasting that night to celebrate another member of the Clan joining the hunters. For ever after that time, the young male carries his knife with him. They are all individual, it would never be mistaken for another's.

My channel asks: what did you call the rainbow? What did that mean to you?

Ky replies:

Do you mean that band of different colours that seemed to throw itself across the sky sometimes when it rained? We had no name for it. It was to us the hand of the Great One drawing on the sky as only he could, using colours that he had, to give us a few moments of perfect pleasure. When someone shouted: 'the colours are there!' we would all run to look at it, to stand in silence and awe and gaze at it, offering thanks to the Great One for giving us such beauty, for there was nothing to equal it in our lives.

Chapter 6 - Death – And New Roles To Take On

Now I wish to break the pattern of the book, for my channel has not asked a question of me to bring this next subject to your attention, for she knows nothing of it.

I wish to talk of the death of my father, the Shaman, and my induction as Shaman of the group. This is important and needs to stand on its own as a section of this book. Please be patient with us.

It was in the time of Sleep when I knew my beloved father was ill, was failing, for there was a hoarseness about his breathing which troubled me much. He was busy with herbal remedies and with honey but these did nothing to ease his chest. I would lie awake in the dark hours and listen to him and cry silent hurtful tears. These were selfish tears for I did not wish to lose the man on whom I had depended throughout my life. But I knew, in my sensible heart, that all will return, all have to return to the Great Spirit at some time in their existence. His time was approaching. Day by day he weakened; night by night his breathing grew worse. During that time my heartache grew steadily and inevitably, deeper until it consumed me. I could not eat; I found it hard to drink and to remember my position in the Clan, the next leader.

Having observed your world for some time now, I understand how the heir to the throne feels.

He knows one day it will be his but before then he has to lose a valued family member to give him that place. And so it was with me.

No one spoke of my future; all were concerned with keeping my father as comfortable as we could. They came with choice pieces of meat, with spring water, with herbs, with flowers for his bedside to cheer him. They came with questions and thoughts, including him still in all that went on in the Clan. This I applauded silently and this I encouraged, for it meant he knew to the very last that he was needed and loved.

Came the morning when I heard the breathing cease and his chest lay still and quiet and I cried my silent tears. I said nothing, I had no need to say a word; all knew that the leader had finally gone to the Great Spirit. They came in silence and knelt in front of our living area, heads bowed and arms folded. Then the Elders came forward and went through the ritual they had enacted so many times before, the taking of the body to the death cave and there leaving it to the Elder women to clean and dress and sew him into the shroud. I did not go with them this time, as I had done so many times before. I stayed in our living area and accepted the tokens of fealty from the Clan members. We had women as Shamans before but not for a long time, according to my father, and he hoped there would not be difficulties when my time came. No one objected to my new role, no one said a word against it. My fear was I was not quite ready but are we ever ready to take on such a huge responsibility?

My channel asked how old I was when this happened. She knows well we had no counting of time but I can say I had begun to bleed, so I was old enough to take on the role of shaman. Just.

I mourned inwardly that I was not there, joining in the chant for my father's passing, not feeling that thrill go through me when the chant began and when it so suddenly ended but a leader has a different role to play. I needed to be visible to those who wished to come and pledge allegiance. And so, when everyone had come to offer allegiance to me, I went into the death cave alone for a long time, kneeling on the cold stone and resting my head against my father's shrouded body. I knew he had been very ill; very tired for some time and was grateful it was over but I felt the loss as if a part of me had been stolen, thrown outside to roll down the side of the mountain and away into the darkness. But then, very slowly, that part which I felt was missing began to fill in, began to rebuild itself. I felt myself grow stronger, I heard my father's voice in my head, whispering 'Ky, be strong, be confident, they will listen to you.' He said it many times and finally I gained enough strength to stand up, my knees hurting, my legs cramped, and make my way back into the main area of the caves.

As I did, everyone stood up. It was not something I expected and I almost burst into tears again, but controlled them and went to what was now my living area and greeted them. The cave broke into its usual noisy self once again, everyone going about their tasks; for the day was well advanced by then and the light was fast fading and much had to be done before we could close in for the night. I remember seeing the fast falling snow just before the men closed the barrier, which had been opened for ventilation for a short time.

Once that was done, the cave was a sanctuary again, glowing with torches, with the huge central fire, with the flash of sparks as knives were sharpened, with the flashes of colour as people moved about and threw things into the fire, things which created vivid flames for a moment or two.

It was then I related our lives to the burned up items, how we lived for such a short time, how we gave off our sparks and colour and then were gone. Relating our life spans to that of the cave, of the mountain we lived in, of the great world outside, of the rhythms of the Sleep and Wake times for us and knew that my father had been one such bright vivid flame that had burned itself out but not before it had contributed much light to the life we lived.

And in that I was comforted.

That night, without any words being spoken, I went to the central position in the big cave and there sat, watching the fire. I banged no stick. It was not right and I was not ready for such a thing. I wanted them to come to me because they wanted to come to me, not because they were summoned in the usual way.

And slowly the Clan came around, as quietly as they could, hushing the young ones who were excited and frightened by turn, for the atmosphere was different and the sensitive little ones knew it and felt it and were disturbed by it.

I waited until they had settled, found a space, huddled against one another for the cave was cold and I shivered in the draught that had found its way to me. I held the cloak around me as tight as I could.

Then I spoke with my people for the first time.

I talked with them of my father, of the great man he had been, of his overwhelming love for me, the result of the passing of his beloved wife, which he had never mentioned in my hearing, but which I knew from the Elder women who had told me of this. I spoke of his amazing knowledge, which he had worked hard to pass on to me, of his abilities which I did not know if I could live up to but I promised them, on his honour and his name, to do all that I could to be the shaman they wanted and needed at this time.

For changes were going on, we knew it. The Sleep and Wake times had slightly changed; there were times when we could not say what the weather would do, where we had always been able to do that. There were concerns that the world we knew outside our cave was changing and we were helpless to do things to stop it or assist it. I spoke briefly of this, for I did not wish to worry them on this saddest of days.

I spoke of his love for the Clan, for all the people both passed and living, of the children which he so loved to watch as they played and grew and became adults, consented to their bonding, held their offspring. Such love was rare; the Clan knew it and venerated it. I vowed to give them the same love, albeit from a woman's stance rather than a man's. My father's wisdom was widely venerated too, and I vowed that I would try and live up to that if I could.

I knew I could speak with the people from other lands, other worlds, for I had done this in private with my father and I spoke of this, which brought a sigh of relief from the Clan who may have feared their contact with these other people had ended with my father's passing. I saw smiles and knew that it was good.

Then, for the first time in my life, I stood up and held out my hands in blessing. The words which came were not mine – they were my father's and they were in his voice.

I do not know who was most shocked, the Clan or me!

It was then I knew all would be well for however long I was Shaman of this group. They knew it too. They all got up, slowly, looking at one another in surprise and happiness, I saw huge smiles, I saw embraces; I saw relief. They went to their living area and the buzz of voices rose as the honey bees' noise built when the men went to steal their honey.

I fell onto my bed and wept with pure happiness. My father had not left, had not been in the death cave longer than the time of light into darkness, but already he was speaking through me.

I felt a hand on my shoulder, turned and saw one of my favourite Elder women leaning over me. She sat down and I went into her arms for comfort, the first of my long day. She held me and crooned over me like a child, told me she would attend to my father for me, asked for the token to wrap in his shroud and then said they would straight away begin work on my robes.

I asked if we could break the ritual and wrap my father in his sacred robes before stitching him into his shroud. She smiled and nodded and I knew then he would be at rest. He became a bigger man when wearing the robes.

I wondered what difference my robes would make to me.

I wanted it to be a while before anyone approached me with a problem, a decision, a question; I wanted to grow into the space my father had left behind. 'I wanted' was a selfish thought and desire and it soon proved to be impossible and impractical anyway. From the moment I rose from my bed until I went back to it at night there were questions and decisions, talks needed to settle this dispute and that problem. I began to fully understand the tiredness of my father some nights, when he could not finish his food and just fell onto his bed and slept. I grew thin from lack of food, unable to eat for I had no time to cook for myself and it had not yet become obvious to the members of the Clan that they had to find something for me if they wished me to survive. It was only when the Elder women came to ask me to go to the secret cave to try on the robes before they were left outside to become patterned that someone recognised my plight. My channel will ask, why did you not tell them you needed to eat? And I will respond, for a very long time it did not seem that I needed to eat for I was sick with worry that I was saying the right thing to the right people at the right time. How could I predict the end of Sleep and the start of Wake? How could I tell them when to put the bull to the cows, the ram to the sharplans and all the other many, many decisions the leader had to make?

Simply put, I lost my confidence and worried instead. Worry made me lose any desire to eat. I lived on pure spring water. It was strange that people thought to bring water to me but not food.

One night, sleepless and restless, I rose from my bed, wrapped a cloak of hide around me, realising how thin I had become by doing that, and went to the solitude cave. I would have give much to have gone outside and seen the stars and communed with the spirit of the moon but I could not move the barrier aside by myself and it would have been unfair on those who were sleeping to make the noise of even trying.

So I went to the tiny cave my father used so often. There I crawled into the softness of the fleeces and let down the hide doorway. All I wanted was to join my father in the death cave. I did not realise or recognise my grief as being the source of my worry, foolish person that I was. I discovered this when the spirits came to talk to me.

For the first time in a long, long period, I was alone. I knew no one would come, no one would try and find me, no one would worry, they would know I had gone to the secret place and would come back to them when the time was right. There I rested, letting the tears flow and mark the cloak I had wrapped around me. Even with that and the soft fleeces, I was shaking with cold.

I said aloud, 'make me warm.'

Nothing happened for a while. I stayed shivering and shaking and feeling ill. Then I felt the cloak begin to mould itself around me even closer, the fleeces seemed to take on a life of their own and begin to get warm. The air in the freezing cold cave warmed so that I could no longer see my breath, as I had before. My body responded by letting go of the stiffness that had consumed me for so long. I had not accepted how rigid I had been, holding myself straight and still and trying to be my father. I let all that go and the tears flowed even faster. Foolishly I laughed as I realised they were becoming hot.

And then they stopped. Not eased off, stopped suddenly as if I had turned them off by blocking them with a stone or branches or something, as I would stop the flow of water in a river.

I drifted in the warmth, seeing Wake in all its wonderful brightness, the great ball of the Sun warming the earth, saw the animals grazing on bright green grass and shoots of all kinds. I saw birds flocking and squabbling and making nests and eggs and knew then how Father could predict when Wake was coming. It was soon. He had gone before Wake but not very much before. I was grateful for that. I could not have stood an entire Sleep without his guidance. After Wake was done, I would have more experience of helping the Clan and not let it destroy me.

And wondered if that was a selfish thought.

Even as I thought that, I heard Father's voice in my head.

"Ky, be selfish. Sometimes you will need time for yourself, as you are now. When you need it, be selfish and take it. Think not of the others. In doing this you will help the others for you will be stronger and ready to help. Make yourself ill and you will be of no help to anyone."

"Father..."

"I know what you want to ask and I will answer you. All you have said so far is right. Now rest, sleep, when you wake, go back to your area and begin the work for which you were chosen. You are Shaman now. There is no going back. Child of mine, know that I will work through you and speak through you when the time is right. For now, you must speak with your own voice and make sure they all know you are Shaman, not just a being for me to speak through. You must be your own self. You must be strong. You must choose your mate wisely. You must – be the child I know I trained and loved and blessed to take over from me."

In that moment he was gone. My head was empty of thoughts that were not mine.

I thought on all he had said and knew he was right. I had to be myself; my leadership was mine, no one else's. But I knew I would be grateful for all he could give me as guidance as we went into what was always an uncertain time. Nothing could ever be assured, weather, animals, grasses, plants, bees; they were gifts of the Nature spirit and could not be demanded.

But I could tell the Clan when I woke that Wake was coming and they should be prepared for it. That would please them. It pleased me.

It was then I went to sleep for the first time in many a long night without worry. My father was safe from his illness; I was secure in my destiny.

I had to hope I was.

The first thing that happened when I emerged from what I thought of as a cocoon was the Elder Women coming to me with food. Fresh cooked meats, leaves, a bowl of warm honey, a bowl of milk. They offered to mix the two bowls and I agreed, for it would be better for me that way. Only when I began to eat the meat did I realise just how hungry I was and had been but had not been capable of eating anything. One held me close for a few moments, saying everything in that closeness that she could not express in words, for to comment on the condition of the Shaman was not something we did.

And then the gifts began to arrive. A child brought me a pebble with coloured lines through it; another brought me a twisted twig that looked like a bat – if you used your imagination. Flowers, carved bowls, beads, braid for my hair, small gifts that meant a great deal. The questions were in their eyes and in their hands but not in their mouths, for only I could say if I would speak to them that night, if I would lead a storytelling time or go into trance and welcome visitors from other worlds. I was not ready for that, my confidence had to grow before I could do that, but I said I would speak that night. They went away content, smiling, waving to one another, calling the news to those who had not come to me.

I rested for a while, replete with food and then braided my hair with the new gifts, added the flowers I had been given, took my stick and walked to the central cave. There, for the first time and with tears in my eyes threatening to fall, I took my father's seat and began to thump my stick on the ground. The first time I spoke with my people I had not used his seat and I had not called them. They had come of their own free will.

They came, pouring into the cave, a never ending crowd of people. It was as if they were all strangers to me that night, I seemed distanced from them, they were people I knew and loved and lived with and yet I knew them not.

The silence became overwhelming as they sat and stared at me and I felt the eyes on me as if they were a physical thing.

So I stood and they sighed as one, a deep sigh of relief. Their Shaman was with them again.

And I spoke of the needs of us all, to work together, to be together, to worship the spirits together and remember those who were not with us anymore. They knew I meant my father and there was another huge sigh, this one of sadness. Then the tears did begin to fall but I did nothing to stop them. I wanted them to know I was Shaman but human too, in the middle of grief for the man who nurtured me and taught me and loved me.

I told them of my father's words, some of them, told them I had seen a vision of Wake and it would not be too far away now and we should be preparing for it, gathering up our possessions which could not be burned but which we needed to take out of the caves, preparing to dig graves for the many who had not survived Sleep, all the things we needed to do. These they knew but by talking of them as one group we became one group, not one leader and a group. I wanted and needed to be part of them, not apart from them. I knew by the smiles and nods and general looks that this had happened, we were one.

Finally I did what I should have done from the start: asked them to arrange for food to be brought to me so I could carry on with my herbal work and all the other things I had to do for the benefit of the Clan. I saw the Elder women nod to one another and knew I would not go hungry again.

And I blessed my people and went to my bed content in my heart and mind that I could do this, I could be Shaman, I could be part of the group and yet not entirely of the group.

And I knew I would welcome Wake when it came, for I needed the sunshine after so much darkness, within me and without.

In the days which followed I found myself doing something I had never done before and in doing it, I realised where my father's wisdom came from when called upon to help in any way in the Clan. I was young, remember that, please, very young, just starting on the time of womanhood, now with the responsibility of the entire Clan, its needs, its problems, its demands for storytelling and advice, resting upon me. There were nights I did not sleep but stayed awake thinking and, most of all, listening.

I have talked about the noise of a great crowd of people living together under a stone roof. In the night the noises are still there, but they are different. You listen to the sounds of those who made future babies, those who were sick, those who were dying, heard their breathing and how it was different from the ones who were well. Heard the babies crying and the young ones calling out in their half-sleep as the night terrors came upon them.

Heard the voices of the animals in sleep or in distress.

Heard the voices of the Clan members who were in sleep or in distress.

I watched the pattern of the Clan during the day, how they lived, how they moved and worked with one another, watched for the aggression I knew was there, looked for the affection I knew was there.

I watched my people and added the day movements to the night noises. I knew then who was rough with their bonded partner in the night time and who sometimes was rough with their bonded partners in the day time, too. I knew who cast looks of wanting on which other person so I was ready when they came for the bonding to be set. I knew who was ill by the way they worked or did not work and knew then who would be laid in the death cave in a short time.

I knew then how my father had been such a good leader, for he had never stopped watching his people even as he took time to teach me all he knew of herbs, of magic, of trance, of speech with the people from other worlds. I knew for I was doing exactly the same thing and I knew too that no other person saw me do it or realised it for it was no more than a glance, a sideways look, a smile here, a frown there, nothing to be noted, nothing to say 'the Shaman watches me' for to do that would be to break the spell that held me in a position of leadership and them in the position of being led.

And I know, even as I dictate this to my channel, that this sounds arrogant in the extreme and almost lordly. But it is not so, it never was so. People are used to being led and some are bound to be leaders and those who are bound to be leaders are the ones who need to be sure of what they say and do and think. And to do that means to observe everything. Not let one tiny thing go by. As I moved through the caves, for whatever reason, I looked everywhere all the time so I knew at any moment how much moss grew, how many animals were in breeding, how many we had slaughtered through Sleep, how much fodder was left, how much fuel for the fire was left, who had not contributed sufficient labour to the cleaning of their area and the consequences of that for their offspring – possible illness. When people live as closely together as we did, everyone had to be careful to remove wastes of all kinds. We could not wash constantly as you do but we could be careful with that which we knew would cause illness, the foul wastes that came from our bodies and over which we had no control, they had to be expelled but they could be removed. They did not have to be in a living area.

And so, a quiet word and once people realised I noticed, they were more careful and considerate of their surroundings and those who dwelled near them and so the incidence of illness fell sharply.

I would wish I could say the incidence of death fell sharply too but we were subject to many illnesses of which there were no cures; even my herbs could not touch them all. And so the terrible hacking coughs would take the old and the young, especially the very young who had no strength to fight the coughs and just stopped breathing. If any ate foods that were not fresh, they would suffer badly through their stomachs and evacuation and sometimes this would weaken them so much they too would stop breathing. There were the mysterious illnesses, the ones where blood came from orifices and we could not stop it or the terrible pain they suffered and they were the ones we sometimes had to stop their breathing to save their suffering. Wounds that turned bad, we did our best with salves and honey cleansing but it did not often cure them. We sorrowed for these for they were our brave hunters who were wounded by the animals they hunted to help with our survival. There were those who seemed to fight for every breath, as if something was blocking them. Again, salves and honey were used but not always helping. We could do so little and that made us, myself especially, feel very inadequate. But we had no knowledge such as you do of the way the body works and what can be done to mend it. I say that and I say I also see how many you do not save, the illnesses which cause great pain are controlled by drugs, not by cure. The end is the same.

Can you see the pattern I am showing you here? It was my given task to be everywhere, to see everything, to hear everything and thus perhaps stop a quarrel before it turned violent, to mediate in arguments over foolish things, to comfort the young ones when they were terrified by the night sounds that came to haunt us. Many a time did I prepare herbs with a young one clinging to my clothes for comfort.

To do this I used all my mind to mind abilities, the telepathy we used so easily, the words that we had and the wisdom of the people from other worlds, those who would come to me in sleep and mention that I should be warned of this happening or that. Always they were right and always I saw my people look at me in awe when I spoke of something they thought was secret to them and them alone.

But I said to them, often, in a Clan like ours, where we lived as one huge extended family, how could there be secrets? With no walls between us but those we acknowledged in granting privacy, the invisible walls outside of which we waited for permission to enter, could there be secrets?

I did think, after a while, that the invisible barriers we 'created' around each living area were so real in their minds that they believed them to be physical and as such hid their secrets from the rest of us, when the truth is, all was displayed at all times. We had no secrets. We had no way of keeping them. Communal living is something you could not contemplate widely today. I see you have communes here and there but nothing of the way we lived, for with us it meant survival. For you it means a way of life only. You could walk out at any time.

And you do.

My channel asks; how did you get through your first Wake?

Ky replies:

It was not easy. Wake seemed to come very quickly but it came with bitter winds and flurries of snow and there were many who said I called for Wake too soon. I told them all I had seen in my vision, the sunshine, the green grass, the newborn and they admitted that there was green grass, there was sunshine and newborns but the ice in the wind killed many of them and stopped us going outside. Now I asked them, how could I tell a wind was blowing that was like ice when I had only a vision?

After that the grumbling stopped and they went out wearing all their Sleep heavy clothes and got on with what had to be done; digging graves, tending the herds, cleaning the caves, searching for firewood and fresh meat. Firewood was not a problem, the winter gales had brought down many branches and trees which were cut up and brought back to the Clan. A good start to the next Sleep, I thought, and I was right. It was one time when we were not almost depleted at the end of the next Sleep, as we had been so many times before.

There came the day when my finished robes were taken outside the cave and laid in the sunshine. Then water was thrown on them and they were quickly rolled up and left. Two days later, when they were unrolled and displayed, the water had left curves that looked like ripples on the water of a still lake. They were beautiful. The beadwork was intricate and delicate and right for a female Shaman. There was a heavy necklace of claws and teeth, set with small stones which had been holed naturally in the earth. The claws and teeth came from animals slaughtered for us to live, the stones were found by the women who searched for such things every time they went out to look for firewood. The stones were treasured for their strangeness and for the way they made necklaces and ornaments for robes.

I took my robes in my arms, they were very heavy, and went into the secret place where I could meditate. I held them to me, crawled into the cocoon of fleeces and stayed there for a whole day and night, at first doing nothing but holding the robes and allowing myself to think of nothing.

Toward the closing of the day I felt a presence in the cave, a close and loving presence but I did not open my eyes. No words passed between myself and the presence, nothing but intense love. Then it faded and another presence came, one of those from another world. It too said nothing but the feeling was deeper, more intense and I know I went into a sort of trance. During that time I know I received much wisdom and it was wisdom I needed. I stayed there all night, resting, thinking and planning. When first light came I crept out and attended to my needs. I knew what I had to do.

The presence from another world had warned me that, being a female shaman, very young and seemingly vulnerable, I had to arrange protection for myself from the Elder men if possible, to ward off the young ones who would attempt to claim me simply because it would make them secondary leader of the Clan, a position they would give anything to gain. This I had not thought of until that moment, not thinking of myself as female and young but as a female shaman, ready to lead. The presence warned me that others would not see me that way. With this insight, I knew I had much to do to protect myself and knew it had to be done in a way that did not seem like rejection of the rest of my people.

And so I made my plans.

First I approached a few of the much older Elder men, those I had known all my life. I approached them as a sort of daughter, pretending to ask for advice and counselling. This flattered them, as I intended it should. I have to say that their advice was good, was sensible and in many instances I acted upon it, which made them even more prepared to help me.

I approached the Elder women and asked for their advice too, things such as would it be better for me to tie my hair up and out of the way so I did not look so young, whether I should think perhaps more of wearing longer clothes to hide myself from view. Again I had good advice which I followed and which pleased them. My channel is not quite asking but I will say now, yes, I did tie up my hair and I did wear longer clothes and it changed the way some of the younger ones looked at me. I knew then that the presence that long night was right in every way.

Of their own accord the Elder men came to me to suggest at least one of them should stay close to me all the time and that they would take it in turns. I asked why and they said, for my protection, as I was a young woman, even though I was their shaman, and that others may try and take advantage of that. It was what I wanted and hoped for but did not wish to ask, for it would have made me look weak and afraid.

Once this had been established, far easier than I hoped, I dressed in my robes and took my father's drum and called my people to a trance session. I felt able to do this, having grown stronger through all I had been told and all I had perceived from my own observations. I sat and banged my drum and they came, eager, excited, so much energy bubbling from them it almost lifted me from my seat. I waited while they settled themselves, while the young ones stopped squabbling and demanding and turned their awestruck eyes to me. It was the first time I had appeared before them fully robed and it made a difference, I could see that. They looked at me with respect, full respect, far deeper than any I had noticed up to that moment. It was frightening for me: the full force of my responsibilities came to me in a wave and I almost walked away. Almost. I sensed my father close to me and knew that I had inherited a highly revered role, one that went back many, many Wakes and Sleeps, far more than could be reckoned or thought about. I felt aged, immensely aged and immensely wise.

No signal was given; it was the telepathy which we shared. The people began thumping their sticks in unison and the sound filled the cave, disturbed the bats which fled as one through their special hole. The dogs looked up, one or two howled and then went quiet. The cats hissed and retreated to caves away from the fire and away from the people and away from the incredible incessant thumping of so many sticks on the solid rock floor, even through the hides.

And I felt myself go deeper and deeper into that magical state that cannot be described. I saw far off places which had colours unlike any on this earth, I saw stars that were not like ours in any way, I saw many suns in one sky; I saw many moons unlike ours, ones that wore haloes of light.

And I spoke with my people. I told them of the great love in which they were held by those from other worlds, those who came to us with wisdom that we could use and be of benefit to our difficult lives, for they knew of our endless struggle to survive. I spoke of the love we had to have for one another, no matter how angry we became for only by being one people would we survive and develop and become better than we were. I spoke of the need for reverence for our leaders, a direct call to my people to protect me as their shaman. I felt rather than heard the sigh which went round them all at those words.

And I wondered how I could hear myself speak when I knew I was deep in trance and I knew I was seeing and hearing it through my father who was standing by and letting me do the trance and he became the channel through which I could see and hear myself.

And when I was through and slowly came back through the layers of consciousness, a word I have learned from your time but only knew then as layers of fog which thinned, became mist and finally became air, I saw every face turned to me and every mouth closed and every pair of eyes shining with love and I knew I had reached them and that was all I needed to know.

As soon as they knew I had fully returned the cave resonated with the sound of cheers and sticks being banged and dogs barking and children yelling, but not in anger, all in excitement and happiness. I saw the big smiles and gave my smile back to them. Then, as one, they moved away from the fire and went to their areas, chattering and waving their hands and communicating in every way they could. The dogs raced around for a few moments and then returned to the fire, lying down, heads on paws, looking at me. I whispered to them that they were my guardians too and had a huff of air from each of them, more than I expected and it was good.

When I got up from my platform, my body was stiff, my joints locked and my robes felt as if they were as heavy as the cave itself. They embodied my role as Shaman and they carried the full weight of the responsibility of the Shaman. I looked down at them and knew they were good. They were very good. They were perfect for me, in size and in design. I loved them and knew that I would wear them with humility and pride.

One Elder woman and one Elder man helped me to my area, telling me how wonderful the trance had been and how much everyone appreciated it. I thanked them both and disrobed under the cover they held for me, so none would see the shaman without clothes. Then I fell onto my bed and went to sleep instantly.

My channel asks, did you make any changes when you were shaman?

Ky replies:

Yes, I did. An important one at first.

I was the first female shaman the Clan had known in so many Sleeps and Wakes they cannot be considered, so I thought differently and did things differently from the men who had preceded me in that role. I brought in a new ritual, one that pleased the women of the Clan very much indeed. After a while, the men agreed it had been an acceptable addition to our lives, but it took some time, nearly all of the first Wake, as I recall.

I brought in a small ritual for every woman who had her first bleed.

For the men this was no more than an indication the woman was ready to be bonded.

For the woman it was an indication that she was ready to be bonded and that she had stepped over from child to woman in a moment of time. The difference was huge, as I remember from my very first time. I recall finding the blood and thinking I was going to die and then remembering what the Elder Women had told me and knew it was a natural thing. But when you are issuing blood, your first reaction is 'I am going to die!' Only afterwards does the natural basis for this happening come to mind and settle the thoughts.

So I wanted a relatively small but important ritual for those who had their first bleed, for the event is a momentous one.

I arranged for an unused cave to be set aside for the young females where they could go for a short time, there to commune with the spirits as they made their transition fully into woman and then to bonding for life with someone in the Clan. These were huge things in someone's life, especially when they are young. We stocked the cave with thick fleeces for warmth and then, critically, we hung thongs on the projections in the walls. We left a basket of stones with holes through them on the floor. The woman who had made her transition chose a stone, one that appealed to her more than the others. She then threaded this onto the thong and hung it round her neck. Then, when she left the cave and rejoined the Clan, everyone knew that she had become Woman and was ready to bond. I noticed that this gave them confidence that I had not seen before, confidence to face everyone and sometimes to walk straight to the person they had been consorting with before the first bleed and hold out a hand. The bonding was made formal from that moment.

I was pleased with this and the fact it made a difference to the way the women looked at me and my leadership. I needed to cement that as firmly as I could, it would reflect badly on me if anything went wrong.

When the first woman emerged from the cave, I heard my father whisper to me; 'I wish I'd thought of that.'

I was pleased but I understood. It was something only a woman could conceive; a man had no idea of the immensity of the change from child to adult with such a momentous thing, the issue of blood.

Another change was the tending of the great fire. For a very long time it had been the responsibility of everyone to tend the fire, to bank up the ash, to cart ash away, to replenish the firewood. As with everything when everyone is involved, everyone thought everyone else was doing it – and they weren't. The fire came close to dying several times in the first Sleep when I became Shaman. I wondered if it was because of my lack of leadership but before I made a move to correct or lecture on this, I watched for a whole day and saw how haphazard the work was.

So that evening I talked on the critical nature of the fire, how we would be frozen to death very quickly without it, how we used it for hot water, cooking and light and praised the fire for being our sole means of being able to live.

Then I asked for volunteers to take on responsibility for various aspects of tending the fire. I asked for one to be in charge of the ash, another of constantly checking the supply of firewood and letting one of the Leaders know when it was getting low, so that when we were able to go out, we would work twice as hard at collecting firewood to bring in.

I asked for a volunteer to cleanse the stones surrounding the fire, to remove any debris and leave the stones clear to cook, so that no one became sick in the stomach with anything they should not have eaten.

Three volunteers came forward and I immediately made them Leaders. That gave them status in the Clan. The applause that met this decision made me see that I did have the right insights into the way we lived together and the safeguard of appointing people to do specific jobs.

And so, another night I did the same thing with the tending of the animals. It worked.

These were seemingly very small changes when written out, but for our people they were very big changes indeed. Status is everything in a tight closed community and each person who gained status did it through offering to serve the community. I noticed they were extremely diligent in their duties and at no time did the great fire ever seem to be on the verge of dying. The same with the animals, they had all the water and fodder they needed and a plentiful supply of ash to cushion them when they stood or laid down. Their droppings were carried away, dried and burned. As I have said before, several times, we wasted nothing.

My channel asks: you were then a woman, did you seek a partner to stand by you?

Ky replies:

My body cried out for the male, for the coupling that brought forth the newborns and indeed a newborn was needed to carry on our line of Shamans. But none I saw were the equal of my beloved father and so I stood back and let life go on, let Sleep follow Wake and Wake follow Sleep and so our Clan prospered and I stood at its head and watched and waited and thought my thoughts. Even in Wake, when all were out, beyond those tending the great fire, that is, I walked every part of our caves, checking, sorting, trying to see if we could organise things better. I put changes in place, ones which worked and the people smiled much and said they were well pleased.

And the young men courted me, coming with small gifts, with smiles of want and welcome and hoped for a response but none was forthcoming.

I looked among the Elder men for a partner, for the young appealed not to me. I sought solace in the companionship of the Elder men and the Elder women, for they had seen much and done much and often directed my thoughts in a way I had not considered and it was always good. I thought one of the Elder men, one whose female had not emerged from the birthing cave, might be perfect for me. We spoke often and I saw the tenderness in his eyes for me. I knew he would be mine if I were to say the words and I wondered why I was reluctant to say the words.

When all seemed peaceful and calm, I went to the cave of sanctuary, rolled down the hide and cocooned myself in the fleeces I had taken there for my own use. I told none where I was going but they seemed to know, fewer people walked the path before the cave entrance and none bothered with calling my name.

There I stayed for a very long time, letting all the worries and cares of my people seep out of me as I first sweated and then chilled my way through a cycle of days and nights. I asked for the spirit of the cave to guard me, I asked for divine help from those who came from other worlds, for I knew not what to do that was right for me and for the Clan and for the Clan and for me, to tell them I did not put myself first. Nor would I.

In the darkness created by the cave and the hide and the mountain we lived in, there came a bright light as in a ball, it gently moved around the cave, it lit upon the bowl of water, all I took with me, it lit upon the bowl for my wastes, I would not disgrace the fleeces on which I lay. It lit upon my hand as I held it out to say welcome and it made my skin tingle and go slightly pink, the colour showing itself in the light of the ball.

And finally it hovered in front of my face.

From it came thoughts. It directed me to someone who was an Elder man but younger than the others, one I had not considered as I was looking for age and maturity and yet, if he were an Elder man, he was mature and had some age on his shoulders.

I knew him well, a good man; a kind man. He was called Jai.

The thoughts came again. I was doing right by my people. A ceremony of bonding would secure that and make them happy for the continuation would be there and they would be at ease in their own minds. I was welcoming to those from other worlds and this would be passed on to others who would come and give of their wisdom too.

The light went very suddenly and the darkness seemed oppressive. I allowed myself to sleep to escape it and when I woke, there seemed to be light but I could see no source for it. Using the light I roused myself, cleansed my face and hands, rolled up the hide and went out to find my future partner and hoped he did not know I was seeking him.

Jai seemed to be everywhere I was, without my knowing how he got there. I found him by my side when I went to get water, when I mashed the herbs, when I visited the sick and elderly, when I checked the animals were properly supervised outside. Always there. The more I saw of him, the more I liked him. He had a gentle smile, a strong face, firm hands, muscles in his arms and legs. I saw him wrestling with a fallen tree; it fell into pieces under his influence, his stone wedges, so fast I hardly saw it go.

This man should and could and would be my bonded partner. If he agreed. I would not pressure anyone, it was not my way. I felt a barrier come between us after a while, one I had to break. I did not love him, then. That came later, when we were bonded, when we were one; when we both stood before the Clan and heard them call us their leaders. Then I looked at Jai and knew I loved him.

The breaking of the barrier was simpler than I hoped.

We got to know one another all through Wake, as we worked toward what I had been told would be a hard and bitter Sleep. I needed his strength and companionship, for I needed to encourage our people –my people – to stock even more firewood than usual, to keep every scrap of hide and make coverings for use during Sleep, to find food, to weave and store everything and anything we would need.. It was a glorious Wake, even considering my newfound attraction, the days were long and hot and the land fertile and giving. We gathered, we stocked, we worked; we dragged home huge trees which had come down during the early part of Wake, when the winds plagued the land. It seemed impossible that Sleep would be as bad as I had been told.

In working together, Jai and I seemed to become one. The barrier I perceived simply went away in the middle of decisions, of frantic stockpiling of everything we could find to keep us alive and well through Sleep.

Then I was told Sleep was coming. Jai knew it from reading my face and knew too what I would do next. We announced our bonding, so that we went into Sleep as one, not two. For the first time in many a Sleep and Wake, the shaman's part of the cave was occupied by two.

The spirits were right. We had a bitter and in many ways damaging Sleep, many trees were destroyed, the waters grew high outside, the snow never came so we had no chance to go out to cleanse ourselves and let off our energy. There were fights, there were problems as any group of people confined to one place were bound to create. Some animals got sick, their meat not fit for consumption. The cats had a hard time keeping the rats at bay.

Some people ventured out, for the cave was a prison to them. A few came back with more firewood, much needed, with reports of deep cracks in the earth and water that flowed ceaselessly and devoured everything. They said nothing of those who did not return and we never asked. It was not good to open wounds of the mind.

Through all of this Jai was calm, diplomatic, strong and determined and made my task much easier. The coverings I had requested were needed, never had our cave seemed so cold, the very walls froze at times and no moisture reached the moss and it began to turn brown. I had to ask for people to sprinkle water on it, or there would be no moss for the newborns or succour for the wounded.

I needed to know there would be moss for the newborns, for I knew myself to be carrying one. My joy and my life were complete.

But not for long. One of the younger men, old enough to know better, young enough to be over confident, began bothering me. His name was Toren. He would interrupt if I was talking to someone, would whistle and make noises during storytelling times; others would send him away from the group or demand his silence which he did, reluctantly. He would make comments about females not being shaman, not being able to rule a tribe. It was obvious he was taunting and testing Jai and determined to challenge his manhood in some way. He was also testing me but for his own reasons. If he desired me, he was so wrong in his choice for I would not go near him unless I had to. Something about him repelled me and I could not do anything about that but try and avoid him if possible. He was good at finding wood for the fire and excellent at stacking it so air flowed through and dried wet wood so it was fit for burning. I entrusted him with this and he did not let me down. If he had only cast his covetous eye on some of the younger available women we would not have had the problems he consistently created.

Jai held out until the beginning of Wake, until there was sunshine and fresh air to cool tempers and quieten inflamed thoughts. It took amazing willpower on his part to do this. But inevitably it came to a fight – which Jai won so easily I knew it wasn't over. Nothing could be over, Toren's feelings had been seriously damaged, some people laughed at him when he walked off, defeated. I was afraid and even more afraid when he confronted me one day and said, well, hissed more than said, 'if I can't have you, no one will.' He then ran from me before I could question his words. I could not belong to anyone else, I was bonded with Jai. Surely he realised a bonding was for life, did he not? That made me fearful for Jai's safety and pleaded with him to be careful, not provoke anything. His answer chilled me, for I had not realised how far he had come in his wisdom and understanding of human nature. He said 'revenge can come in many ways, most of them silent. There will be no confrontation with Toren again, he will be afraid of losing a second time. Watch what you do, beloved one, for he may take his revenge on you rather than me. Or so I am told.' And in that moment I knew if anything happened to me, if I fell sick or had an accident, Jai would lead the cave dwellers on into the future. It comforted me even as I feared giving up the life I loved, even if it was fraught from morning to night with decisions and problems.

I asked for guidance on why I feared giving up my life, asked what was going to happen to me and had no answer. It was not for me to know.

My channel asks, how long did Toren hold out before taking his revenge?

Ky replies:

So little time, too short a time. My love child with Jai never saw life. It was half way through Wake, when my newborn was showing under my clothes, when the 'accident' happened. I wonder even now if it was the sight of the newborn bulge I carried that sent Toren crazy. We had dealt with such obsessions in the past, Father and I had coped with them. Sometimes the people had quietly walked away in the dark and we never saw them again, sometimes they walked away but stayed in our area and tried to be friends with our clan. It didn't work.

Toren knew all this but was too involved in his own feelings to see how it was damaging others.

I knew he was doing something. Collecting water was a ritual; it took the same time every time. Nothing to think about, nothing to consider. Walk to the spring, fill the container, return. I noticed sometimes he was slow to return and wondered what would hold him in the dark cave, nothing but the sound of the water rushing over the rock, nothing to see, nothing to do but fill up and return. I didn't consider it often enough or important enough to check if all was as it should be. I had so much else to think about, the start of Wake is the busiest time of our lives, the animals rushing in all directions as they celebrated their freedom, checking our supplies and restocking the wood as fast as we could, so much to do.

Which is why when one day I decided to collect water for Jai and myself, I never gave my safety a thought. I knew someone was following me, I heard the rustle of clothes and the sound of rasping breath but as with so many things, I never thought anything of it.

I filled my container with water and turned to come back when the roof of the cave entrance fell down on me. I had time to shout Jai's name and then there was only blackness.

Everything else I tell you now was seen by my spirit, for I was crushed under the stone.

I was looking at a mist of dust and stone fragments which quickly settled. The water was contaminated by the dust. I remember thinking we needed to find another water source and where would we find one so easy for us to reach. I also remember feeling a sense of tremendous loss as the realisation occurred that the way back to the caves was completely blocked. No one would find me; no one would bury me in my robes. I tried to cry but nothing came. I called for Jai but no sound came.

Time passed. I stayed staring at the untidy mess of rock which had come down. It was dark, if there were marks where someone had loosened the stone I could not see it but I knew, as surely as if he had stood before me and admitted it, that Toren had set this up for the roof to come down on me. Then it would seem like an accident, not a killing.

I know not, even now, how long I stared but slowly I thought, I am spirit, I can go where I wish and yes, in a moment of thinking it, I was the other side of the rock fall and there my heart broke, if a spirit heart can be said to break. Jai was on the other side pulling at the rocks, with others trying to stop him for fear of more roof falling in and more lives being crushed. I watched helplessly as Elder Men finally led him away to our small area. I heard voices, I heard wailing and barking, the dogs had been roused by the noise and the emotions.

I looked for Toren and saw him on the very edge of the group wailing and crying at the great fire. Saw him edging to the entrance and slipping outside. I knew, in that moment, they would never see him again. No one would. In doing that he shouted his guilt to them all.

Jai was inconsolable. Great sobs shook his body, no one could comfort him. So they let him be, just stood watch should he hurt himself in any way, watched until he fell into a troubled, exhausted sleep.

The next day Jai spent the entire waking time saying over and over 'my love, my child, have gone.' No one could get him to say anything else or to stop saying that. They let him mourn in his own way.

The third day he got up from our bed with a new look; determined, courageous, sad all together in one set face. He looked round at the gathered group. 'Find me Toren,' he said first.

'He is gone, Jai, he left the day it happened. Why?'

'Because he did this in his rage not to have the one I loved.'

A sigh rippled through everyone and a look of understanding appeared on all the faces.

'Then it is our task to go on without Ky and without the child. She has come to me in my sleep and told me what I must do. At dark we will sit round the fire and mourn together for our loss. Tomorrow we go on as always. Sleep will come; we will need to be ready.'

Then I watched with spirit tears pouring down my face as one by one each person in the Clan came to touch Jai, shake his hand, offer a kiss, offer their devotion and help.

And one by one they built back up the man I loved. I knew all would be well.

AFTER TIME

One Sunday I was visiting my friend Terry Wakelin and was in his garden by a pond which had water running endlessly through pipes. As it fell back into the pond it seemed to be speaking to me, the words were almost there. I could almost taste them.

Later that evening, working with Ky, she told me how she had learned the language of water. I knew then that it was her influence that afternoon, waiting to see if I could hear the language, too. I almost could and if I'd had sufficient time, I might, through meditation and concentration, speak the water language. Unfortunately the pond was not mine and the weather was not always clement enough for me to sit there for any length of time and learn a new language. I listen for it endlessly, though, water pouring from the tap, running down the drain, it all has its own message. We just choose not to hear it.

Ky went on later to talk to me of the language of the wind and rain, of the trees and bushes. Only then did I realise how much we take for granted – and ignore – in nature.

Ky also confirmed what I had known for some time: I am claustrophobic in narrow low roofed caves. Ky is one of my past lives.

www.ingramcontent.com/pod-product-compliance
Lightning Source LLC
Chambersburg PA
CBHW071955170626
46813CB00005B/1889